VIRGINIA HAMILTON

TIME PIECES

THE BOOK OF TIMES

SCHOLASTIC INC.

New York   Toronto   London   Auckland   Sydney
Mexico City   New Delhi   Hong Kong   Buenos Aires

No part of this publication may be reproduced, stored in a retrieval system,
or transmitted in any form or by any means, electronic, mechanical, photocopying,
recording, or otherwise, without written permission of the publisher. For information
regarding permission, write to Scholastic Inc., 557 Broadway, New York, NY 10012.

This book was originally published in hardcover by the Blue Sky Press in 2002.

ISBN 0-439-51714-1

12 11 10 9 8 7 6 5 4   6 7 8 9/0

Printed in the U.S.A.   40

First Scholastic paperback printing, January 2005

To Arnold

To Leigh and Jaime

CONTENTS

CHAPTER ONE

My Dad Says to Me

"There's nothing like the stars tonight, no sir," Valena's dad said to her. They sat close on the top porch step of home. Valena sat on one side of him, and Laddie, their big dog, sat on the other side. Laddie had his paw on Valena's dad's knee.

Valena took her dad's hand and bounced it in her hands. "Well, what's it like up there by the stars?" Valena asked, but she already knew. She just wanted to hear him talk.

"Probably real hot and real cold, Valena," he said. "Not one man has gone that far."

"Have any girls like me ever gone up as far as a star?" Valena asked him, but she knew better. "Any moms?"

Her dad laughed. "You are teasing me! But no, not a girl nor a mom that I know of."

"Good! Then I can be the first." Valena grinned in the dark. She started an old joke they had. "Hey Dad, what's the *matter*?"

"Atoms and protons," he said.

"And neutrons and quarks."

"And strings," he said.

"Strings? Don't know about them yet."

"You will," her dad said.

Katydids and crickets were sounding everywhere. Stars were hanging in the trees. Valena giggled. "Stars are twinkling fireflies in the leaves."

Valena heard other things in the dark. "Dad? But what's that blooping?" She scrunched closer to him.

"That's the sound of tree frogs," her dad said.

It scared her, but she didn't say so.

"Afraid of night noises?" Her dad read her so fast! "Not my Valena."

"I can run clear around the house in the dark," she told him, just to show him she was brave. "Can I? I'll take Laddie with me." *Say no! Say no!* she secretly begged him.

"Bet you'll run the night clear around and beat it, and scare it. You're that fast."

Valena knew he was grinning in the dark. "You'll beat Laddie, too. Go ahead!"

All at once, the night turned awful. The dark shape of a ghost rose in the yellow-light grass. It grew. It moved. It . . . it . . . was coming! Valena's breath rattled. Her stomach turned, and she couldn't breathe. "Dad?" She saw Laddie get up and stand still.

Her dad sighed. "Valena," he said to her, "don't scare yourself so much. It's only your mom, walking near the window in the lamplight." He pulled Valena's fingers from his arm.

Ohhhh. Valena was trembling. She felt it in her shoulders and down her back. When she could finally talk, she told her dad, "I wasn't afraid. I'll chase the night some other time." Her, Valena, embarrassed. "I'm too tired now." She leaned her head against her dad. He patted her arm as her mom came and sat with them.

Valena felt like an onion. Her mom peeled her from her dad's side. Then she felt like a sweater, as her mom folded Valena to her chest. Valena snuggled in. Her mom talked. Valena felt cozy, looking up; her eyes felt full of starlight.

Laddie came around, got a pat from Valena's mom. He lay by Valena's side. She placed her arm around his neck. He put his head down and panted once, like sighing. Both of them were sleepy all of a sudden.

Valena's dad was small-talking with her mom in his man's deep voice: "Need to dig up more potatoes. Did the children polish the tomatoes?" Her mom: "Well, yes, a whole bushel they polished." Her dad: "Beefsteak ones are the best growers; we'll sell them to Hyde's Market. They'll take three bushels." Her mom: "Oh, that's good!"

Valena didn't listen much. She closed her eyes. Next thing, her dad was lifting Valena and taking her into the house. Him, telling her mom: "She weighs light as a feather. She's all bones." Her mom telling him, "She eats, but not the vegetables. Because you won't eat them."

Valena's dad took her up the stairs. "Fresh night air," he said to her. "You'll sleep hard this night!"

Next thing, Valena was in bed. Heard his footsteps going.

She yawned. *I am going. Sleep.*

CHAPTER TWO

The Day of the Bored Alice

"Go get the milk," Valena's mom said. It was after their supper of fresh corn, string beans, rice, and chicken. Lemonade, too, and berry pie. *There's nothing better than milk with berry pie,* Valena thought. *We drank up all the milk.*

"I'm full, and I need a walk," Valena said. She loved going to get the milk.

"Well, go with Babysis, then," her mom told her. "It'll be dark soon."

"Not until after nine," Babysis said. "Plenty of time to visit."

"Oh, we know how you love to visit with Tonya!" their mom said.

Babysis was not a baby; she was four years older than Valena. Her real name was Geneva, which she did not like. When she was born, Valena's brother, Adam, was a year old. He said, "I have a baby sis!" And that was how people called her — Babysis. She told Valena that when she turned eighteen, she would change Geneva to Beverly.

Babysis let Valena hug her and lean on her. She read to Valena sometimes and let Valena braid her hair. Babysis was like the sun in the morning. She came over to wake Valena and kissed Valena's cheek.

To get milk, they had to go down the lane, across Wyandot Road. Where they lived was rural — fields and farmhouses and small add-onto houses like theirs. Valena's dad had added a front porch and a back porch. He said that one day he'd close the front porch into a screened-in one. *That'll be the day!* thought Valena.

To get to Tonya's, they turned down Gravel Pit Road. Tonya's dad and mom, Mr. and Mrs. Price, had a bigger farm than most. Valena's family didn't have cows, but the Price family did — a whole line of cows in a big barn, and machines that milked the cows.

But first, before they got the milk, they visited Tonya. Well, Babysis did.

Tonya was a really pretty girl. She was the same age as Babysis, but she was taller, with gray eyes and honey skin, and all the boys liked her. Babysis was best friends with Tonya. They both liked the boys and whispered and laughed a lot. They were always fooling with their hair and telling each other, "Here come the boys. Just don't let them see you looking at them!" But they stood right there where the boys could see them. Valena thought Babysis and Tonya were *strange*.

Some people got their milk from Mr. Price in

bottles, but Valena's family got theirs in a silver can with a high handle. Valena and Babysis covered the top of the can with cotton cloth, and they always carried it home that way. That can was heavy!

It was the time Valena's dad called twilight and her mom called dusk. It was the time after Laddie went to meet Valena's dad and walked him home. Each evening, Laddie waited for Valena's dad to come off his afternoon job in town. Laddie went down the road to where it forked with Limon Street. Everyone called the fork "the Point." Laddie waited on the grass at the Point, looking down the Dayton Road, waiting for Valena's dad. And when he saw her dad coming way far off, he crossed to the other side of the road and ran up there, fast as he could.

Laddie ran and leaped high and stood, paws on Valena's dad's chest. He waited to be petted. Then, they walked home. Laddie walked at Valena's dad's side, just as smooth and proud as you please — both of them, dog and man, with heads held high.

Valena helped Babysis get the milk can ready. Valena called this time of day "Come on, Nightly!" *Ha! Ha!* She knew she loved it, whatever it was called. There were streaks of purple and red and orange from the sun going down. She waited by the barn for the girls to stop whispering so they could all go home. A minute later, Laddie found her. He was panting. Valena patted his head to calm him.

Babysis and Valena carried the milk, and already Tonya and Babysis were talking again. Valena thought they were talking about the boys playing night baseball in the town park. Later, she thought, they would sneak away to the park.

"What do you think about that, Laddie?" Laddie stopped his panting and made a sound. He lifted his head as if to say, "Yep, I think so, too."

Valena watched the sky, ready for all the pretty sun streaks to fade away. Then, Nightly would come. *Maybe Babysis and Tonya will hurry the milk home. Then they'll sneak away, and I'll follow them,* she thought.

They put the heavy milk down for a moment, and Laddie lay next to Valena. His panting slowed. Valena waited, watching everything. She loved this time. She listened, all around. Birds quieted down. Nightly, Nightly, was coming.

Something. She didn't know. She watched it up there. The sky looked somehow brighter tonight. *The streaks are getting louder in their colors,* she thought. *It looks like . . . the streaks . . . the streaks are moving. Seesawing and swinging. Bouncing. They are shivery.*

Valena watched them grow crimson and glow in flames. They went in and out, strong and quivery. She couldn't take her eyes away. She watched and watched.

All at once, the sky was full of the streaks of the sun — so many streaks of light, moving the way the church organ sounded. *Loud and fading,*

rising and falling. But glowing greens and blues.
Valena felt smaller and smaller, looking at them.
The sky is growing — all wavery and weaving. The
sky is magic!

Valena got to her feet. Laddie stood, too.
Valena was yelling before she knew it. "Babysis,
everybody!" She jumped up and down, screaming. Laddie looked at her and backed off. He
woofed at her once, standing there.

"Everybody, look up! Look up!" Now Valena
was frightened. She held her mouth closed with
her hands. *It's like the sky is falling! It's coming*
down in giant colors!

Valena filled up with tears. *The colors are*
hanging down in moving curtains of sky. It looks
like I can touch all the curtain colors.

Laddie walked back and forth across the road.
All around Valena, he walked. *He's guarding me!*

Somebody come and hold my hand! Please? "Are
the sky curtains going to cover me?" Valena could

barely talk. She sat down in the road, too ashamed to shout what she was thinking: *I'm scared!*

The tar and gravel road was dark and smooth, still warm from the day. *Nobody hears me, either. It feels as if the sky is screaming at me, in great scary colors.* She felt smaller every time she looked.

She stopped looking.

Now, folks were coming outside from their houses. Valena could see them off through the fields. She got up. Her legs were full of ticking. Everybody looked to the sky. Laddie was standing close at Valena's side. *Good dog!*

"What is it?" Tonya yelled. "Oh, my goodness!" Looking up, she turned round and round. "Is it the Lord?"

Some boy came running, yelling all the way. "Bored Alice! It's the Bored Alice!"

"What?" Tonya asked him.

Now Valena saw who the boy was. Bobby

Twosons. His family had a farm of wheat fields and hogs.

"Bored Alice, Bored Alice!" Bobby Twosons shouted. "Bored Alice! My teacher told us about Bored Alice once."

Uncle Dell McGill came down the road. Valena's dad's brother. Melinda's dad. "Where's Melinda?" Valena managed.

"Scared, in the closet," he said to Valena. And he said to them, "Now I bet that sky scared you some, too." They were all scared silent for a minute.

"Uncle Dell!" Babysis called out. They ran over to him. Uncle Dell was short and round.

They were all beside him, touching his arms. "Uncle Dell!" They held his fingers. Valena leaned on him. Everyone was looking up at the sky. But Valena didn't look. Laddie leaned against her.

"It sure makes me dizzy!" Tonya said. "Never seen anything . . . what is it? Is it the Martians?"

Uncle Dell smiled. "Nope! It's called the aurora borealis," he told them.

"Bored Alice," Bobby Twosons said.

"The aurora borealis is also known as the northern lights," Uncle Dell said. "We rarely get them this far down the states. The northern tier of states gets them more."

"That's up at Cleveland, I bet," Bobby Twosons said.

Uncle Dell smiled and nodded. He went on, "It's also known as the aurora of the Northern Hemisphere. Science doesn't know why it is, really. It has to do with sunspots, they say. It sure is a grand treat of nature."

Our uncle Dell McGill is almost as smart as my dad, Valena thought.

"My teacher says it's Bored Alice," said Bobby.

"Well, you maybe mis-heard her," Uncle Dell told him. "The way people will mis-take your own name." He grinned. "People hear your last name as Two Sons, only it's spelled T-o-u-s-o-n-s, like it's French, one word. Only, maybe one time long ago, it was, like, two sons." Uncle Dell paused for a minute. "So go ask your teacher again," he finished.

"I'll do it," Valena said. "I'll go by Mrs. Tate's house and ask."

"Better you than me," Bobby said, under his breath.

Almost at once, asking Mrs. Tate went out of Valena's mind. It seemed as if it took a long time to get home. Babysis had her arm around Valena all the way. Tonya came with them, to help carry the pail of milk. But then she remembered, "I'll have to walk back home all by myself."

Valena had stopped looking up because all those bright sky curtains coming down scared her so. She only looked at the ground. But Babysis was looking up as she walked.

"Is it still there?" Tonya asked.

"Still there," Babysis said.

"Oh, goodness. Hope it's not the Martians," Tonya said again.

"It's not anything but nature," Babysis said. "Laddie will walk you back home."

"What's he going to do if one of those sky curtains comes falling down on my head?"

"Laddie isn't just a dog. He's a good, smart dog," Valena told her.

"Nothing will hurt you with Laddie there," Babysis said.

Nothing will hurt me, Valena told herself.

"Oh, okay then," Tonya said.

They all believed in Laddie. They went on down the road. The sky was beautiful and something awful, full of moving colors above them. *I can't get clear what it is doing. It has never done this before. It has always been our spacious skies, getting dark, getting light, raining, snowing. Nightly, Nightly. Never like this, making us so small, so scared under it,* Valena thought.

Tonya and Babysis held on to Valena. Laddie knew that something was up. He looked at the sky and barked a couple of times. Then he looked straight ahead. Valena could see his shoulder muscles when he paced. *The Nightly is that bright.*

Bored Alice couldn't make Laddie whimper. Couldn't fool Laddie into running ahead of them. All over town, dogs barked. Been barking; Valena just now heard them. *But Laddie, big dog! Laddie sure knows what is what.*

At Valena's house, Tonya began to cry. She was afraid to walk back alone. Laddie was sitting down, and he wouldn't go unless Valena's brother went, too. Adam was waiting on the porch.

"I bet you taught Laddie to do that," Babysis told him, "and I know why!"

"Well, I don't. What are you talking about?" Valena asked Babysis.

Adam jumped down from the porch. "Come on, girl," he said to Tonya. His voice was soft.

Laddie stood at his side. He went with Adam and Tonya out of the yard to the road.

"Scaredy-cat!" Adam told her. Valena couldn't hear what Tonya said back. *Something.*

"Oh, brother!" Babysis said.

It looked like Adam was holding Tonya's hand. *Goodness.*

CHAPTER THREE

Mrs. Tate

Valena didn't remember to ask Mrs. Tate until Saturday. "My pea brain!" she told her cousin Melinda. "I forgot till now."

"Well, I'm not going over there with you!"

"Well, who asked you to?" Valena told her.

"So, so?" she said back. And made dust rise, doing a fast wheelie.

Why does she always come bother me, first thing? Valena thought.

"Why did you stay in your house when the sky looked all crazy? Were you scared?" Valena yelled after her. Melinda pretended not to hear. "I know where you . . . hid!" Melinda's bike wobbled. Valena held her breath, but Melinda didn't fall. She went on home, not looking back.

Well, I'm glad to go by myself, Valena thought. *Mom made a babypie that I can take to Mrs. Tate. Babypies are just smaller than regular. This one's minced berry; she made it when she made the regular.*

Valena took a babypie covered in a napkin. She put it in her bike basket. She knew to ride slow and careful, straight up the road. It was the time before folks finished their chores and everybody came inside. Time when kids minded their own business and folks were thinking about a nap.

Valena got there, and Mrs. Tate came near the front-door screen. "Go around," she said.

I guess she doesn't want children tracking up her parlor, Valena thought. *I've never been in her parlor. You go into parlors, sit down, when you have something to say. That's why you bring baby-pies, too. Maybe she doesn't see I've brought her something.*

Valena went around; she followed the path to the right. There was a side door and veranda. Mrs. Tate came to the side door. She had two red circles on her cheeks. She had the same red on her mouth. Her hair was kind of orange-yellow and gray. *Mrs. Tate lives by herself,* Valena thought. *I've never seen Mr. Tate.*

"Mama sent this babypie, Mrs. Tate."

"Well, I never," she said, opening the side screen door. "Thank you. Thank Harriet; thoughtful of her." She took the pie.

"Can we sit in your parlor?" Valena asked.

"Oh, child! For heaven's sake. Come on in, and we'll sample this bitty pie!"

Valena followed her. Her kitchen was all right. She had them sit at a table that had a pretty yellow tablecloth. She cut them both pieces of pie. They had small glasses of lemonade.

"Did you see the sky the other night, Mrs. Tate?"

She grinned, sucking on pie. "Oh, my, yes! Wasn't it grand?"

"The Bored Alice," Valena told her.

"What?"

"The Bored Alice." Valena said it again. "S'what Bobby Twosons called it. Said he got it from you, that you said that's what it was. My uncle Dell says it's an aurora something."

"Well. Dell McGill is right, too," she said. "But that Bobby!" Mrs. Tate laughed. Her eyes nearly closed. She wiped her mouth and took a sip of lemonade. "Well, heavens, he means aurora borealis; that's what I told his class."

"Well, he said you said Bored Alice," Valena explained. "I thought it sounded funny, too. That's why I came. I know Uncle Dell sounded right. He said Bobby mis-heard you."

"Bored Alice, well! But they're all like that. Hear you plainly and look straight at you. Injuns will still get it wrong, like they never heard a word." She said it in a quiet voice, sounding only a little bit hateful.

But Valena's mouth went still. "They're called Indians and white people," she blurted out. "Those are the proper names, my dad told me."

Valena held her lemonade with both hands. Stared at the pretty necklace Mrs. Tate was wearing. It had a white cameo. "Kids always like to pick on the Twosons' little boys," Valena heard herself say. "And they want to fight with Bobby Twosons and his sister, Renda Twosons. But those kids are both tough, man!"

"Awh!" said Mrs. Tate. She slapped her napkin on the table.

"Kids like to pick on me, too, sometimes." Valena said it before she knew how to shut up.

"Who picked on you?" Mrs. Tate asked. Staring at Valena with her eyes wide. "You're so light, nobody would . . ." she left off.

Valena didn't look at her. But she named them

aloud, who picked on her. Some girls from town. "We were coming home from school, all of us together," Valena told her. "Then, they whispered and pulled away, and ran, and called me a bad name."

"And what did you do to them?" Mrs. Tate exclaimed. She didn't look nice at Valena, either.

"I ran after them?" Like a question. "I was mad at them? They ran up on Miss Baily's porch," Valena told Mrs. Tate. "We all take piano from Miss Baily. She came outside. They were talking to her. She hollered for me to get on home."

"And I think you'd better just do that," said Mrs. Tate. "Here." She got up and scraped the rest of Harriet's good pie into her garbage.

Valena felt just awful all of a sudden.

Valena got up to leave. She didn't look at Mrs. Tate because it hurt so that Mrs. Tate had thrown out her mom's pie. Valena knew Mrs. Tate was pointing at her. Because Valena was heading for her parlor.

"Not that way!" Mrs. Tate yelled, really loud. "The side door!"

But Valena flew through Mrs. Tate's parlor. Valena touched her velvet-green chair with sticky fingers. Valena flumped down on the humpback couch all cushiony soft. Valena pumped up and down on it before Mrs. Tate could get to her. Then, Valena was outside, unhooking that front-door screen of Mrs. Tate's and slamming it behind her.

"You, Valena! I'll tell Harriet!"

That's Missus Harriet McGill to you, Missus Tate-er! Tater Head!

Valena found her bike. *I'm Valena McGill, too! And my mom's a Harper. So there.* Valena picked up a rock. She wanted to throw it so hard it would go right through Mrs. Tate's window and find a velvety seat in her parlor. *It will say, "Valena was here, Missus!"*

Valena let the rock drop to the ground. Mrs. Tate saw Valena ride fast down the street. Valena rode past her own house. *Figure she's called Mom by now, too. I'm in trouble!* So Valena rode on and on, until she got scared all by herself out in the farmland. She looked for Bobby Twosons's house.

No, think it the proper way, she told herself. *It's Bobby T-o-u-s-o-n-s.* Valena saw his house far off the road among fields.

We'll ride his horses — he and his sister, Renda, and me. I daydream it: They let me join them and their people because I can ride a pony. We will hunt a good day. We will find it.

Valena turned her bike around in the hot roadway. The air was stuffy and still. She got some of the steam out of herself going home. She almost got cool, from the little breeze in her face.

Valena rode easy into her yard. She coasted under the big maple and slid off the seat. Fell on her stomach and lay there in the grass. Breathing hard. A drum in her head. All quiet at a time of rest. *I wonder if Mrs. Tate called Mom.*

Mean Tate! Just had to make me go to the side

door. *And not the front door. I hate that. Dad and Mom never do that. We don't in my family. All kids and grown-ups come in the front door.*

Once, a baby pig had come in the front door. It was the day of a home visit from Valena's teacher. Valena's mom was embarrassed. Valena felt dumb and poor, to have a pig in the house.

Now Valena smelled the green grass and closed her eyes. *I imagine ponies, and me, and Bobby Tousons, riding bareback.*

Imagine I tell him all about the side door and how Tater Head said how I am colored light. And what she said about him: "Injuns . . . they're all like that."

Bored Alice and injuns. In her mind Valena repeated it to Bobby and snickered.

I see us, quiet a long time. I see us riding far. "Aurora borealis," *he says.* "And Indians, or Amerindians — not injuns." *At last, he grins.*

"And Mrs. Tate. Not any Tater Head," *I tell him.*

We nod, grinning all down the road. We are sure

we have everything right now. "My dad says you have to let it ride," says Bobby Tousons. "My dad says Mrs. Tate is from the old school."

I think about that. "Different kind of school than now?" I ask him.

"Better school now than then. You can paint outside the lines now," he says. "And you can make all kinds of color combinations outside the lines." He whistles through his teeth.

I think he means this: Everything won't have to be a certain way. Means, more than one way and not a bad way. A good way.

I see the day right with us; it's shining on us. We trot, cooling the ponies. "We will win the day," I tell Bobby Tousons.

Sitting tall, he says back to me, "We already did."

CHAPTER FOUR

"The Greatest"

Valena was excited. She'd been beside herself since two nights earlier when her dad had come home with Laddie yipping at his side. Laddie knew something big was going to happen. He'd jumped around Valena's dad, just like a kid full of a secret. Valena's dad probably told him on the way home. He often talked to Laddie when they walked together. He would say things like, "Well, Laddie boy, how was your day? Did you get a good bone?" And Laddie would pace along, talking back in dog *ruffs* and *yips* and looking up at

Valena's dad. They just about always had a good talk on the way home.

"Too bad, Laddie can't go. No dogs allowed," Valena's dad had said.

"Go where?" her brother had asked him.

"Why, to the circus. The Ringling Brothers and Barnum and Bailey Circus."

"No!" Valena's brother had said.

"The circus!" Valena had hollered.

"No!" Babysis had yelled.

Valena's dad had said they would take two cars. Neither one of Valena's folks ever drove a car. Melinda thought that was a riot. Mr. Henry often took Valena's parents into the city when they needed special shopping. "Valena, you'll ride with Uncle Dell's family. Adam, you and Babysis and Tonya will come with me and Mr. Henry."

"Tonya's coming . . ." Adam had begun, but he didn't finish.

"I knew Babysis would want her friend along." Valena's dad had smiled at Adam.

Adam had looked away. Babysis had grinned at the ground.

Tonya! Pretty Tonya! was what Valena had thought.

And that was that.

It was two days later, and they were going to the circus. "Today! Can you believe it?" Valena asked Babysis.

"I think I almost do. Because we are almost ready," Babysis said to Valena.

Valena got all dressed up in her Sunday clothes. Wore new sandals with socks. Hair held back with barettes and made into a braided ponytail.

All by herself inside herself, Valena felt as if she were the only one going. Even though she was squeezed in the middle, she fell asleep in the car. But so did her cousins Melinda and Cynthia. They woke up all at once. And they were almost there.

"They're right behind us," Melinda said. "Mr. Henry's car, with all them in it."

"Where?" Cynthia and Valena asked at the same time. Cynthia elbowed Valena and turned so that Valena couldn't elbow her back. Valena wouldn't say ouch, although Cynthia's bony elbow had hurt.

They parked in a lot with a pack of other cars. A block away they could see lots of people lining the street. And . . . *elephants*.

"Hurry!" Cynthia said.

Even Uncle Dell and Aunt Demmie had to hurry. Valena's dad and all of them were right together. Valena's dad told her to stay close. "Always keep one of your family in sight," he said. And she did, too. Most of the time, Valena's dad was right there with her. Cynthia and Melinda were together. And Babysis and Tonya were with Adam.

Tonya held tightly to Adam's arm. He acted as if he didn't notice.

Babysis and Tonya were jumping up and down, trying to see over people's heads. "Cut it out!"

Adam scolded them. "You're breaking my arm!" But he didn't look mad. He eyed Tonya a lot.

Valena's dad squeezed everyone through the crowd. Valena could see all the elephants now. There were parading circus people, too; beautiful ladies, some riding the elephants. An elephant made a loud horn sound, and the whole crowd fell back. Valena held her dad's hand and never let it go. *This parade is sure something to see.*

"Well, what'dya think?" Valena's dad asked her.

"It's just a great thing," Valena told him. She smiled up at him. "Oh, Dad!"

He laughed, then said, "Quite a show!" and talked excitedly to Uncle Dell. "We're kids today," Valena's dad told her uncle.

"I know it," Uncle Dell said back.

Valena couldn't talk because of seeing so much new. There was a closed truck with a really fat lady painted on its panels. And a giant man was so tall, too tall. Maybe on stilts. He had a midget lady in a long lace dress, riding sideways on his arm.

People all around couldn't get over how tall he was and how small she was.

"Do you believe that?" Uncle Dell said. "Height of eight feet, I bet."

Valena's dad laughed. "Believe it," he said.

"I believe it," Valena piped up. "I see it before my own eyes!"

There were all kinds of circus folks and circus animals. Some horses, with men riders standing on them and doing back flips on them. There were trick dogs walking on their hind legs. They were led by a trainer, all dressed up, in a top hat.

"Laddie should see the dogs!" Valena told her dad.

"He'd probably lead them all home to share his supper," her dad said to her.

All the time, a loudspeaker on a car blared out, "The Greatest Show on Earth!" and told what would happen later in the seven rings under the "big top."

"Came in on four trains," Valena's dad said,

"with one hundred and seven carriages and freight wagons."

Down the street came a cage, bigger than anything.

"Cage ninety-eight," Valena's dad was saying. "It's longer than anything."

Ninety-eight was covered up in canvas. It had three strong men on each side, and one in front, and one in back.

The street crowd quieted down as the cage came by. The loudspeaker car didn't say a thing. The strong men kept their eyes on the crowd and their arms folded. In the covered cage, something was making a lot of noise. The crowd was hushed. And the cage went *BOOM! BOOM!* Like something awful was trying to break it down.

"They won't let you see what's in there yet," Valena's dad said to Valena.

"They make you wait and pay for it," Uncle Dell said. "That noise is just a boom machine. The *Big He* ain't in there, I bet."

"Oh, sure he is," Valena's dad said. They argued a moment.

But what's the Big He? Valena wondered. She leaned on her dad and looked up at him. *What is it?*

The cage on wheels was moving slowly. A tractor was pulling it. Valena looked at the curvy blue words on the cage cover.

GARGANTUA! was written on the canvas. *The Largest Gorilla Ever Exhibited. The World's Most Terrifying Living Creature. GARGANTUA the Great. The Greatest Ape of All!*

Then, all of a sudden, it was as if nobody else were there — just Valena and her dad. And a crowd she didn't know. No Melinda and Cynthia. No Adam, or Tonya, or Babysis. Valena didn't know where they went. It was Valena and her dad, that's all. Not even Uncle Dell.

We are in this big crowd, inside a place like a building, underground. It has long hallways, wide ones. How did we even get here? So much to see, I can't take it all in. This is bigger than any inside-place I've ever seen.

Valena's dad bought tickets, but she didn't even turn to look, didn't even think about it. The crowd was pressing in tight, and the cage was up above on a platform. The cover was still on it. The *BOOM, BOOM, BOOMs* were coming out so fast. People were acting up, trying to get as close as they could. Valena's dad held them off with his back and arms. He said, loud, "People are beside themselves — no manners at all!" The pushing crowd let up.

I'm too small in the crowd, in too tight. But Dad is close. Still, I'm shaky. Afraid I'll throw up. My stomach feels empty. I only had Mom's corn mush with syrup and milk for breakfast, and way early, too. She didn't come. She told Dad, "No thank you, I can't stand crowds."

Valena could see pretty well around folks' shoulders. And she peeked around their arms.

"Take that cover off!" someone shouted.

This great big room is packed now. We all have to stand. There is nowhere to sit. There is just all of us and that loud, spooky cage. And fusty odors that make my nose itch. And make me sneeze.

All at once, the cover slid down the back of the cage and was off.

Stone silence. Quiet, the way trees are silent before a big, bad storm. Dead still, like all of them were waiting for trouble, standing there looking.

The greatest, the biggest, the hugest! More than any animal Valena had ever seen. More than any great wild beast of the world. A grand, giant animal with long, dark fur. Gargantua! With a face so terrible — big and crooked. To Valena, it was all beyond what her brain could think.

But I know about apes. We all come from them, don't we? Apes were there in the days of old, and some-us were there. And they went one way, and we went the other on the human tree. All of us primates. Isn't that so?

But what do I see in front of me, in this biggest cage of glass with heavy bars on the outside? It is the Big He, the most awful and hair-raising animal in the world. The greatest of all gorillas. A beauty of a Gargantua. People beside me say he is the grandson of other fabulous gorillas.

Gargantua is so tall he almost touches the top of the cage. He is looking, staring at all of us. Bigger, broader than any man in that basement room. His giant head turns back and forth and out over us. His eyes are shiny, deep red, like blood.

I can't help jumping up and down. I don't know why. Just clapping my hands and jumping. Until his head swings around. Gargantua. Sees me.

Valena felt a rush of ringing in her ears. She couldn't hear anything. Cold chills spread down her back. *His eyes are like nothing I've seen. His face is all misshapen.* Valena's dad grabbed her arm. She stopped jumping.

They all just gazed at the great animal.

He must've seen me jumping. He took hold of the bars and pulled them and pounded them. Gargantua threw his head back. He barked, on and on. He pounded his chest: "Bomke, comke, gomke!" It sounded like a drum. He screeched and howled. Valena had to cover her ears. People backed up. Everyone was told to leave by a man in a uniform.

"Time to go," Valena's dad said.

There were animal smells underground that took away Valena's breath. They hurried out. So many people — all of them moved away. The awful stench of the animal area hit Valena hard. It stayed in her nose when they got to the big tents. They were out of the smells up close, but at the circus, everything stank as if it were the raw of life.

Later, Valena saw high-wire performers. They were awfully good, but it was hard to look up so much. She and her father had pink cotton candy, spun in a machine on a paper cone.

Valena saw the fat lady up close. Her fat spilled all over, even over her tiny feet. Valena saw the rubber man, who could twist himself every which way. But mostly the great Gargantua was in Valena's head.

They went home, and Valena was almost sick in the car from the hot dog and ice cream she had eaten before they left. And it was Nightly, Nightly, when they got home. And dark of a new moon.

For a long time after, Valena dreamed about Gargantua. No, they were nightmares, her mom said. Said to Valena's dad, "I don't know why you had to take her to see such an awful thing."

Her dad said, "Well, she loves to see. Better to see than not. Even see scary. . . ."

Gargantua would come into Valena's dreams. He'd walk in the yard. Valena would call for Laddie as loud as she could. But Gargantua just kept leaping and hurling into the lilacs, and barging all over the place. Valena would flap her arms with all her strength. And she would rise higher than he could reach. It was so hard to stay up in the air. But she always did. And Laddie was a little, scared puppy.

Gargantua flung Laddie. Then, Valena would wake up crying and screaming. But she didn't care. *I mean, I do, but I'll tell you this: I will always love the scary sight of that greatest wild animal. I will never forget him. I will always admire him and worry over him in my rememory.*

Later, in the papers, Valena's dad read a story about Gargantua. The animal's face was all ugly because a mean sailor threw acid on him, on the boat that brought him from the jungle.

I bet Gargantua never wanted a cage, even a great big long one. Who would? Well, I sure wouldn't. He only wants to be outside in nature. He's like I am. He wants to be free.

CHAPTER FIVE

The Women's Volunteer and Reckon Society

Simony drove up in Aunt Demmie's car, with Cynthia sitting next to her. Valena's mom and Aunt Demmie were in the back seat. Another car pulled in behind Simony, with three more from the WV and RS. Their church's Women Volunteers ran the Goods Exchange — where folks gave old clothes. The women made the clothes like new and supplied them free to people who needed them.

Once, Valena was given a "special" — a velvet

dress from the GE. But that didn't happen often. Her family could usually afford new clothes.

Volunteers like Valena's mom, and Aunt Demmie and Aunt Claire on her dad's side of the family, met once a month at someone's house. They kept track of the profits of the Goods Exchange business. And they wrote down the order of "Reckons," they called them, stories told of past times: "To respect those gone before us by our account of their thorny road north."

One of the volunteers would stand and tell about "one time of a poor soul from long ago." And another would write it all down in a lined notebook. That was usually Simony's job.

"Hope they don't drink up all the pink lemonade," Adam said, now. He and Valena were outside with Melinda and Laddie, next to the house in the side yard. Their mom had said if they kept themselves out of sight, they could stay in their frayed, summer play clothes while her company was there.

A full-grown lilac bush largely shielded them anyway from the two cars that had pulled up. The women got out and went inside, not knowing what was going on in the side yard.

Adam was trying to teach Melinda how to walk "up-wrong," as he called it — "instead of up-right," he explained.

Valena could do it a little bit already. Adam was shirtless, looking all tough-muscled while walking on his hands. He could walk clear across the side yard and back, up-wrong, like that.

"Do it," he told Valena and Melinda. "Just get on your hands and point your toes up."

Well, it was easier said than done. They tried. Valena got her legs almost straight, but then she fell sideways.

Melinda sprang down, with her hands and arms spread wide. Trying to push herself into a handstand. She went over on her back every time. Then she and Valena got the giggles.

"Shhh!" Adam warned them. Just beyond the side yard, the women sat in the living room.

Melinda and Valena grabbed Laddie. They hid their faces in his long fur to keep from laughing out loud. Poor Laddie whined and shook them off and stood on his back legs like he would leap in the air. They petted him.

"He thinks he's just like us," Adam said. "He'll never know he's a dog." Adam took up the hose and put cold water in Laddie's bowl. Adam drank from the hose as Laddie drank from the bowl.

"Let's play statue," Melinda said. "I can't do the up-wrong."

Adam didn't answer. He finished drinking and gave a soft whistle, which was his call to Laddie. "Run!" he whispered. And he and Laddie took off.

It hurt Valena's feelings, the way Adam could take off with Laddie whenever he felt like it. Cut her out of play, like Laddie didn't care about her at all. Out of the yard and across, going toward fields and open land. Both of them just loved to run. *My smart-aleck big brother!* Valena thought. Now they had nothing to do. They couldn't play statue with just two people. Melinda had stretched out on the grass, with her arms over her eyes.

"Don't go to sleep," Valena told her. "You might miss something."

"What, the bees buzzing by? Huh."

"Well, you think of something to do, then," Valena said.

Melinda was quiet a moment. "Don't know," she said, finally. "We could play jacks, but we don't have any."

They'd taken the jacks to school, and now they were missing. "How about going inside?" Melinda said.

"Yeah. See what's going on. I'm getting hungry for something, and I'm thirsty, too," Valena answered.

It was quiet inside the house as they slipped

in. They found a pitcher of lemonade and a plate of left-over sandwiches on the kitchen table. Cheese spread with lettuce on whole wheat. Two halves of chicken salad. They each had one of those.

Trying hard not to make a sound, they filled paper cups with lemonade and sat down at the table. They ate and drank. Everything tasted really good. They were hot and sweaty, but cooling down now.

It was all real soft talking in the living room; listening hard, they could almost hear. When they were done, they wiped their faces and hands. They got up carefully, and went closer.

Most of the women volunteers were good tellers. Valena's mom was hostess this time, and it sounded like she was talking. "What's she saying?" Melinda whispered.

"Don't know!" Valena said softly. They crept up to the living room archway and hid against the wall dividing the two rooms. They didn't dare peek around the wall, but they could hear all right.

Valena's mom, Harriet, was saying a piece about some past reckon. She had to be standing at the far end of the living room by the piano. At this end of the room, Valena could hear the scratch of pen on paper. Had to be Simony, writing it in the notebook.

Valena and Melinda sat behind the wall, resting their heads against it. Valena listened with her eyes closed, to hear better.

"She was thought to be a child when she got there," Harriet was saying. "But that was before folks knew she wouldn't grow."

Melinda nudged Valena to say, "What's she talking about?" Valena didn't turn; she shrugged, meaning she had no idea.

"Why, what do you mean?" Aunt Demmie asked Harriet.

"I mean it's told that she never got any taller than she was when she arrived there. I'm getting ahead of myself," Harriet went on. "Martin Rothford had gone down to Savannah, and they say he met one of the last ships at the port. Some few Africans on it, little ones, too, and she was one of them. When he took her to his home, she became a secret on the Rothford Planterland for a week. Only Martin Rothford and a few of his trusted helpers knew she was there. But the boy, Perrin Rothford, Martin's son, discovered her.

"Young Perrin was called 'Spindly' by the Occupants. He was such a loose-jointed, skinny child. Smart, though. Smart and sharp as he could be. He was ten or eleven then.

"Now. I call *them* Occupants," Harriet said. "Those were owner Martin's 'poor unpaid workers' who were our relatives. *Never* call them slaves, no indeed. And never call men like Martin Rothford masters. No, sir! No. He was the owner of the unpaid Occupants."

Harriet sniffed once; Valena heard her and knew her mom had her nose in the air.

"There were maybe fourteen, fifteen of the Occupants, and others, too, who were not our relatives. Maybe more. Not all of the relatives found their way here, after Spindly kept his promise and managed to spirit the girl and some of the Occupants out of the South to the North. A dangerous undertaking. The girl was grown by then. It was after Spindly had gone off to the seminary. The war was going full tilt. And owner Martin was glad to see his Occupants go. It was near the end, you see, and freedom was on its way."

"Aunt Harriet, where do you get these tales?" It was Valena's cousin, Cynthia, sounding amazed and unsure of the truth in them.

"It's not a tale," Valena's mom explained. "It was handed down from Luke himself. My granddad. It's what we know and reckon is the truth, for it came from him, and this far. It's been brought through many different times by some of us who want to tell and keep an account. There is more than one account of the same situation. There always is. But who cares? This is the way we tell it. This is what we know and keep close."

"Now mark my words," Harriet added, "before the war started, the African, Tunny Maud, was taken to Virginia to live and toil on the Martin Rothford 'possession,' they called it. Known as the Rothford Planterland — I already said that. And here's the account of it."

Harriet took a deep breath and continued. "Tunny was the only recognizable word the little African seemed able to say. Well, it sounded like Tunny. Could've been anything — Tunnee, Tundna. Who can say for sure? But Tunny stuck. It was easy for Martin and his crew. And she said it over and over, Tunny, Tunny-tunny, like a song. Martin named her Tunny Maud but often called her Dim Tunny because he came to believe she was stupid. Oh, but she wasn't! And yet he was taken by her, some say. Quite struck, and caught by all the strangeness about her. And so was his wife. She was Sarah Ann Rothford. Tunny was to be her house servant. That would be the day!"

There was a long pause from the other side of the wall as the group in the living room took in Harriet's words.

Valena opened her eyes. Whoever Dim Tunny was, she wasn't about to be the maid for anybody. That's what her mom meant.

And then, her mom told — Dim Tunny.

CHAPTER SIX

Dim Tunny

Martin thought she was two years old.

She peered at them, grinning, for she saw through him and his men. He, Martin Rothford, thought her a baby. True, all the way in the boat, across the big water, they had kept her with the other little ones. Black-as-tar totties, is what the boatmen called them. Some, like her, were not so black, but more reddish brown. She heard the words but didn't know their meaning. She simply knew they, the totties, and herself, were thought of as little monkeys.

She was born among the great trees of the

forest, under the forest jungle canopy. It seemed all like a dream now. A tree was planted for her in the first month of her birth. She counted nine or ten more plantings over her years.

She'd run away, hiding for so long. She had been so afraid, she couldn't think which way to go. When men with nets came stealing, she lost her way. She lost count.

She walked forever, eating what she could find. The forest always fed her. But she had to sleep. She had dropped down from tiredness, just for the length of leaf shadows moving to and fro. She folded herself within the shadows. And was caught on the ground. Men with nets, skilled with catching such as she. They herded her with others they had caught. She and the others were forbidden to speak.

This last pale chief now commanded her. And she was taken away from the trees; she was bought and sold like a monkey. Would they cook her and eat her like the traders did, like a monkey?

He was called "Boss" or "Marsah" or "'Yassuh." He talked gibberish. He rubbed at her brownish-red skin. Her hair was matted flat to her head. He had her put in a covered cage on a wagon. She fought those who handled her.

"She is filthy and smelly. Awful-looking child, ain't it?" Martin muttered. "But there's something about it." He sensed that this little tottie was peculiar. For she seemed all energy and light. Out of her ugliness shone the biggest eyes he'd ever seen on a tottie. She was like a featherweight as she bounced off the bars of the cage.

He took her up and threw her high, and wouldn't let anyone catch her. She sailed down and spun on one foot and stood still, as if the ether had taken hold of her and made her land solid as a rock.

Martin would find out what kind of knack she had. What flair. For he was certain she had one. And then he might sell her and turn a profit.

Once they arrived at the Rothford Planterland,

they kept her far away from the great house and the cabins. Unsuspecting, Martin and his trusted partners, the driver's helpers — these were blacks — and the overseer's side men who were white, quickly made a makeshift corral around the so-called child. It was like a sturdy pen for baby pigs. It was strong enough to keep a tottie in. It was placed near a neglected and over-grown path by the forest. They had no idea what part of the black continent she'd come from.

They poured sun-warmed water over her, soak-ing her good. It was a hot day. She had on a form-less shift to her ankles. They had no chains on her; just a neck rope, which one of the driver boys held on to.

Martin meant to have the child taken to Myree, the old woman of the cabins, to have the child properly cleaned by hand. They could tell she hated strong light. It hurt her, somehow. They needed to get the fright out of her and to stop that soft jabbering she did.

All the way from Savannah, she blabbered and babbled some god-awful gibberish of *Tunny, Tunny.* Striking her head and beating herself around the chest. Every time she could grab a leaf, she stuck it to her clothing. And screamed softly, if that were possible. With her, it was; she sang, *"Tunny, tunny, tunny, tunny,"* on and on and over and over. *"Tunny, tunny, tunny, tunny."*

Just like a little monkey. Look how fast that baby can move. Fast and prankish.

"Quit that jabbering! If you don't quit, I'll teach ya how!" Martin yelled.

She wouldn't. "Tunny, Tunny!" So he had a boy wrap a cloth around her mouth. She soon soaked the cloth with her saliva, her spit; she gagged, and got it loose.

That first day, she leaped over the low corral and climbed a tree. Heading for the surrounding forest. It took them the rest of the day to catch her and build a cage.

They sicced the hounds on her. Keeping her to

several trees. She caught a squirrel and held on to it like it was a doll baby. She screeched, in a low throwing of her voice, for she seemed to hate loud noise, "Tunny, Tunny, Tunny!"

When Martin's boys climbed two other trees and held poles with nets on the ends, she came down. By this time, the whole Planterland knew something unusual was taking place.

She scooted down, still holding on to the squirrel. The squirrel never moved against her. And for Martin and his boys, that was not only odd, but impossible. But it was, because they saw that it was. A wild, forest squirrel letting this bitty tottie handle it.

"Gives me an idea," Martin murmured. "She needs something to hold her in. But I don't want to punish her too hard."

Spindly was wandering the Rothford Planterland in the time before supper, when all was fairly quiet and the sun hadn't quite gone behind the endless forest. All the cabin folks were in their home places or in their street, where they cooked the food they ate. And where they talked and sometimes laughed. Spindly could go over there before dark, if he wanted to. His muma and papa let him have the run of the Planterland. He would sometimes tell the black boys he played with that he was their Yassah. They didn't laugh. They'd look around and pick up stones and lope them at him. He let them. He cherished them. They were the only friends he had.

Spindly was on the lonesome path near the forest, where he hoped to see a ghost. The black boys said they'd run into terrible sights whenever they got too close to the forever forest. Spindly suspected that what frightened them was just some of his dad's men trying to keep them away from the trees. For the forest was good cover for runaways escaping north.

He'd inspect the area and have something to tell them. But before him, above the path, was a sight that froze Spindly to the spot. Something above the path. Nearly over his head before he saw it.

There it was. A cage made of bamboo. A child, swinging in it. A squirrel with a red neckscarf, leaping around. And leaping on the child's shoulder. The shock of it all caused Spindly to fall to his knees and fall back.

The squirrel now stayed still on the child's arm when it saw him. Spindly did not move. She, the child, did not move.

"Tunny!" she seemed to gasp in a kind of harsh whisper that sailed into his ears.

He scrambled up. She jumped high and landed softly. The squirrel watched him from its arm perch.

Spindly and the child watched each other. Unmoving, mindless. Just looking and watching. Spindly shivered. The child shivered, mimicking and mocking him. The squirrel's tail went around and around.

He'd never seen anything like the child. "Tunny!" she said deep in her throat. He sat up.

"Tunny?" he said back. He'd noticed something. When she said, "Tunny," she put her hand straight up, with thumb on her chest.

He did the same and said, "Spindly."

"Spynin, Spynin." A peculiar sound. She was trying to say his name.

"Yes! I'm Spindly!" he told her.

"Tunny, Tunny!"

"And you are Tunny. How did you get here?"

She grinned. "Tswa-Batswa," she murmured, again, pointing thumb to her chest. "Tunny!"

"I don't know what you're saying. But I can help. You want down?" He pointed down. Saw where a rope attached to the cage was wrapped around a stake in the ground. It took him a while, but he managed to get the rope off the stake. Carefully, straining a bit, he brought the cage down.

Now they were on the same level. "I can get you out," he told her. *What am I doing?* he wondered. *Why am I doing this?*

She stared at him. Dressed neatly in a sackcloth with a red apron. And slippers on her feet. *Where'd she get that getup?* he wondered, looking her over.

And then she said, "Myree."

"Oh, ho!" He laughed. "That old woman did you up so dainty? Must've taken to you. She don't like most totties. . . . Are you one?"

Seeing him staring at her, she circled suddenly in a startling, graceful twirl. She let the squirrel go. It leaped from the cage. She grabbed the bamboo bars and shook them, like she would tear them down.

"Wait, I'll get you out. Wait!"

She leaped and twirled; leaped and twirled, until Spindly thought his head would spin off.

"Tunny, Tunny. Tunny, Tunny!" Whispering. Something about her. Swiftly, he grasped that

her prancing was her wish to be free. "Let me out!" her leaps seemed to call to him.

"*Tunny, Tunny!*"

"Keep it low," he told her, "or you'll have the whole Planterland out here."

There was another rope that held the cage door to the cage height. It was fixed so she couldn't reach it from the inside. Spindly climbed atop the cage. It took him time, but he got the rope untied. He lifted the opening back and slid it off the cage.

Tunny stepped out. She was so little, and agile, too. Before he knew it, he was sitting, watching her leap and sing.

"No, no! Shhhh! You'll have everybody here!"

The sun was going down. "Shhhh. The quarter will finish supper, and they'll hear you!"

She wouldn't stop. Her prancing and leaping was such that she must've been a performer of some kind. She could flip on her back, and then forward again. She could leap three feet off the ground. Hands locked to her sides, she could lift one leg and the other in a fast, step-whirl from side to side. She did amazing moves with her hands, arms, and feet.

Tunny was dancing to the leaf shadows in the forest. She could gaze over there and see them. And she could copy them. They made her less alone.

The girl could do anything, it seemed to Spindly. "You're no tottie!"

She could do anything but keep her voice down. It could be throaty, like a bullfrog. Or it could be high and screeching. She did a dance, bending, reaching her hand and arm down. She murmured strange sounds. Her hands mimed gathering food. And another act, clearly someone shooting high up in the trees. She was a perfect mimic!

Before long, the Occupants were there, creeping up on the cage as if it were alive. They saw the girl and crouched to watch. For she still danced, springing on her hands now. She could move on her hands as well as her feet. Her feet seemed not to touch the ground.

"Batswa, maybe," Old Myree murmured. "Pygmy little girl."

"Ahhh," came from those who watched. Someone brought her food. She ate eagerly.

"So she's not a tottie; I said not," said Spindly.

Before deep darkness fell, some of the boys helped Spindly get her back in the cage. She wanted to go with Myree. Myree put her hand on her, covering her face. She told her, "Give it time. You got to take what is given. It will get better."

She listened to Myree. She looked around at all of the Occupants. Spindly stood among them, the only one with pale skin, light as the moon, all over him. She reached for him and rubbed his arm.

She studied his ivory moon light, but it wouldn't come off.

They put her back in the cage; she let them.

They secured the opening. They hung her up off the ground, just the way Spindly had found her in her prison. Yes. She was a prisoner.

My papa did that to her, he thought.

She settled down. She said something. But they didn't understand.

When the others had all gone back to the cabins, Spindly stood there in the darkening night.

She knew he was there. She sat quietly inside. The squirrel was back with her. Spindly couldn't see it, but he heard its sounds, like a chicken clucking.

"I promise you," he told her. "Tunny, I promise. One day, I'll make you free. And all of them others. Black boys. Free."

He left her. He heard her as he left. *"Tunny, Tunny, Fuh. Feer-y, Tunny."*

CHAPTER SEVEN

GA Peavy
Tells a Tell

Valena went with her mom whenever her mom took baskets to kin shut-ins. Today they were going to see Valena's GA Peavy. Her mom said GA Peavy was dying slowly.

"How slow is slowly?" Valena asked her.

"Slow enough to give me a fit," her mom said.

"What kind of fit?"

"Kind like exasperation, from her telling me, 'I'll *go* when I'm ready.' And she will, too."

Means, die when she's ready. GA Peavy. Gives me the shudders, thought Valena.

They went on down the road. GA Peavy lived farther out of the way than they did. Valena's mom had goodies in the basket. Some cold chicken, rutabaga pie, and some creamy potato salad.

"Everybody dies." Valena felt wise, saying that.

"Some folks have more fun dying than anything," her mom said.

"GA Peavy!" Valena said.

"It keeps your GA Peavy busy — living! Here. Take this basket. It's pulling on me."

All the cousins called Great-Aunt Peavy "GA Peavy" because to say Great-Aunt Peavy all the time was just stuffy. *It sounds put on, for sure,* Valena thought.

GA Peavy lived in a little house with a small front porch where she used to sit. But the car traffic got too much for her, so she moved to her covered back stoop. Then, one of Valena's family — it was cousin Simony — really got to GA Peavy.

Valena held the basket with both hands and skipped to the gate and opened it. GA Peavy's yard had more shade plants than grass and more weeds than anything. "Mom, come on! Let's get it over with," Valena whispered.

"You know you enjoy yourself!"

Valena couldn't help grinning. She opened the door and stepped inside with her mom right there after her. The little house was shut tight, with blinds drawn over the bright day. It was hot and dry, without a lick of air moving.

And there was GA Peavy, smack in the middle of her living room.

Her four-poster bed took up all the space between the couch and her rocking chair. "Why are you still in bed?" Valena's mom asked her.

"Easier for visiting," she told. "Me, lying up here, and them, sitting on the couch or in the chair."

"You're a disgrace," Valena's mom said to her. GA Peavy seemed not to mind. She grinned at the room, knowing she'd gotten Harriet's goat.

"Aunt Peavy, you need to get up more and go outside," Harriet said.

"Nonsense," GA Peavy said. "Want me to catch my death? And the coydogs to eat me?" She stopped a minute but then went on, "I'm going to tell Simony if she doesn't tie up her animals, I'm going to shoot them!"

"Simony hasn't been here yet?" Harriet asked.

"Has, too, and I almost didn't let her in," Peavy said.

"She might've opened a window," Valena's mom said. "And you might've got out of bed."

"Huh!" Peavy said. "I was up, and now I'm back!"

Then she went on about Simony. "She and her mama, feeding all the stray dogs and cats and chipmunks. Harriet, nobody else feeds them along the road. They come clear down here, squirrels and groundhogs, and expect Christmas from me every summer's day! I tell you, this place is overrun with vermin and varmints. Something's got to be done."

Valena's mom sighed. "Aunt Peavy, you know very well none of that is true."

Valena's Great-Aunt Peavy was Harriet's father's sister. Harriet's dad and mom were no longer living. They didn't talk much about them. It made Valena's mom too sad.

Now, Harriet went about her business, putting her basket goodies in the refrigerator. Valena put a small pile of clothing in the washer the way she was supposed to. Somebody else would come and hang out the clothes. GA Peavy liked to get up and get her own food whenever she felt like eating. The family just took turns doing what had to be done for her.

GA Peavy pulled her small self up higher in the bed.

"Why, the animals are eating me out of house and home! I threw breadcrumbs to the birds. The chipmunks had them before I turned away. I went to shut off the back porch light last night, and lo and behold, there was a whole pack of raccoons begging at the door! Looking like bandits. Just awful."

Harriet nudged Valena. So she had to speak up. "Good morning, GA Peavy," Valena said, as if she'd just come in. "It's a sunny day outside. You want to jump in your wheelchair and have me run you around the yard? I won't let anything get you. You can even use the walker instead, if you want."

Peavy was silent a while, looking to one side of Valena. "Oh," she said finally. "Child, I don't *run* anywhere anymore. And I never know who's here for real, either, and who's not."

"I'm here for real," Valena piped up.

"What's real, anyhow? I'm sure I can't tell," GA Peavy finished.

"Aunt Peavy, now don't," Harriet chided her.

"Don't what?" GA Peavy asked. "Don't tell that

folks come and go in here like it is a train station? Whether they've been in their graves or not?"

Valena sucked in her breath. *Ghosts*, she thought. *GA Peavy thought I was one!*

GA Peavy rolled over, and Harriet and Valena helped her into her chair.

"You're all dressed!" Valena piped up.

"Well, why not?" she said back. "Think just because I lie down, I don't get up and dress myself?"

"Oh," Valena said. Harriet smiled at her and put a finger to her lips.

"That child's great-grandpapa, Luke Harper, was here last night," GA Peavy told Valena's mom. Harriet looked uneasy.

I know that GA Peavy's Papa Luke, Mom's grandpapa, had a funeral, thought Valena. *I know what's what. She means a ghost. Luke, my great-grandaddy!*

Valena sat across the room in the rocking chair. Next to it was a nice table full of things GA Peavy had collected. There was an iron elephant, smooth and cool to the touch, and very heavy. It was Valena's great friend. "Hi, Nimbo, hi' you today?" said Valena, only moving her lips. She took up Nimbo and held it tight.

"I was a little girl," GA Peavy was telling. "My brother, your mama's Uncle Dandy, was a boy. We rode horses for Horneby's Food and Carryback. We took lunches from stores to the laborers all up side the Darke County and down the country, and then some. We both rode bareback and barefoot for hours, carrying baskets full of food, strapped to the sides of the horses."

The sound of GA Peavy's voice took Valena at once to a time she'd never known but could picture when GA Peavy spoke. Just the way Valena could when her mom gave a tell.

"We carried milk and water to folks who couldn't get around much," Peavy was saying. "Commence, little one!" All at once, she was talking to Valena.

Valena made some noise, and her mom put a hand to her back and shoved Valena forward. She sat on the bed right there before Peavy. Valena was almost bigger than her, and she wasn't comfortable being so close. She had her hands deep in her pockets. She could feel GA Peavy's breath on her arm and smell the medicines on the side table.

"See that picture on the wall?" GA Peavy asked her.

Valena nodded. "It's a place a-fire," Valena said. She'd seen it before, and she knew what it was. "It's . . . somebody was on fire."

"It's where Papa Luke got exploded." GA Peavy's voice changed, sounding like an echo in a far place.

"That's not quite the way it was," Valena's mom said.

"Now were you there?" Peavy asked. She waved Harriet quiet and went on: "Brother Dandy and me, why, we rode the horses to Wendt's Station every day, taking deliveries and carrying some back. It was one day, we were finished and clomping our horses up and down and around the field at home. Maybe we heard something, and maybe we didn't. When you ride, it's hard to know whether it's the horse or the ground under it that's shaking. But quick, someone came running and hollering: 'It's the powder mill! Swoosh!'

"Well, Dandy and I heard it, I think. But everything happened so fast. Our mama had heard it. 'You and you!' Mama screamed at me and Dandy. 'Your papa! Get him! Get Luke!'

" 'No, wait,' Mama told us. She ran inside and came out almost at once with a can of salve for the burns."

GA Peavy stopped. Her eyes roamed around the room as if she saw something moving. Valena's mom was still, and so was Valena.

"What happened?" Valena asked Peavy.

She stayed silent a moment longer. "The fire.

It burned down the powdermill. We brought Papa Luke home. His hands, his chest, and his arms were burned, although he was covered with black soot from the fire, and his hair was singed to the bald. Put the salve on his hand, for that was all we thought was burned. When we got home, Mama bandaged his head and hand. And cleaned him all over, and saw his back and arms were bad. She got a doctor, finally."

"Bandaged his hand closed," Valena's mom said. "So that it grew that way, the skin of his fingers attached to his palm. Never opened his hand after that. Folks just didn't know any better."

GA Peavy snored softly, sound asleep. She was the fastest sleeper in the world. "Why didn't she finish the tell?" Valena asked.

"Once she sees it, remembers it all, she no longer has to tell it, I guess," Valena's mom said. "She's content that she's brought it back, seen it, remembered it, one more time. I'm not like that, though."

Valena stared at GA Peavy, and it was as if no shriveled old thing like her could ever even have a parent. Children have parents and grandparents, was what Valena thought. But then, GA Peavy did look almost like a child. A child left out in the sun too long, or something. All dried up and wrinkled, like a youngun.

Valena and her mother went home. Halfway there, Valena's mom was looking hard at her daughter. Valena almost stopped because Harriet was looking down at Valena's hands. She still had them in her pockets. Moving one of them around and around. Surprise! Something cool and heavy was there.

Harriet stopped Valena, jerked her daughter in front of her. "Valena. What have you got?" Said so softly, Valena knew she was sunk. She'd forgotten; just clean forgotten.

Valena's mom took her daughter's hand out of her pocket. She pried the sweet little iron elephant from Valena's fingers. She hissed at Valena and jerked her around. They went back the way they'd come to GA Peavy's. Valena hung back. Harriet jerked her arm.

"I forgot!" Valena cried.

"You did not forget," her mom said. "You may *think* you did." When they got there, Harriet knocked once, and they went in. Peavy stared at them with bright eyes. Right on the table, right in front of her, Valena's mom placed the elephant.

"She took it," Harriet told GA Peavy. GA Peavy stared at Valena.

"What must I do with her?" Valena's mom asked.

Peavy held out her hand to Valena, cupped big enough to accept the cool elephant. Valena went up and placed it in her palm. Tears rolled down Valena's face. She covered her eyes.

GA Peavy brushed Valena's arm down. It was as if she'd hit the life out of Valena. "Don't you come back 'ere till you're an honest woman. What'dya say to that!"

"I . . . won't," Valena stammered. "I'm sorry!" Valena felt just awful.

Then, they left, Valena and her mom. They walked all the way home. Never said a word. And never spoke about what Valena had done. It stayed with Valena all day — what she had done — and it became all mixed up with her Great-Grandaddy Luke's burning. Not a minute went by that Valena didn't know she was a little thief. Later, she went to her mom in the kitchen to lean against her. She put her arms around her mother's waist, and she wanted to cry out, *I just forgot about it!* but she didn't.

Valena's mom held her, said, "Shhhh, now." But that was all. Never said, *I know you forgot.* Never once.

Then, Valena went and sat in the living room. All by herself. And fell asleep.

CHAPTER EIGHT

Why Valena's Uncle Rafe Went Down to Ripley

Valena's uncle Rafe Harper was her mom's brother and Cousin Simony's father. Valena liked Cousin Simony, always had. Uncle Rafe was mostly silent, like Simony. But he never talked to Valena. *I'm just a kid*, Valena thought. *He talks to Mom and Dad sometimes. He looks at me sideways, like he does at all kids. I never heard him talk to Simony. But he can look at her, and she knows what he means by it. He tells tales on a*

Sunday visiting and laughs at his own tells. I like to listen.

Once, Uncle Rafe told about the "petrified" man, he called him. There was a funeral, and Uncle Rafe said that all of a sudden, the man in the casket sat up. Shocked, the funeral-goers hollered out. Uncle Rafe said the man in the coffin was "mortified" to find himself where he was. The man was "soundly petrified," Uncle Rafe said. Meaning, Valena guessed, that the man was just scared to *death* — *ha! ha!* And when Uncle Rafe told it, he acted it out. He stood stiff as a board. He fell over like a two-by-four. Said the "petrified" man had done that when he found himself alive in the coffin. And as Uncle Rafe performed the dead man's fall, he caught himself on his hands about two inches from the floor.

Valena's mom was not at the funeral. She said only Rafe saw the deceased sit up like that. Melinda told Valena it never happened because

Uncle Rafe made it all up. Still, Valena wished she'd seen it.

Every year, there was a special something that Uncle Rafe did. When Valena heard about it, she never asked why. Because it didn't seem out of the ordinary. It was just something Uncle Rafe did once a year.

It was a warm morning, about 10:30. Time when the road was quiet, and cars of Field traffic had gone on to work. That was Wright Field, the Air Service Command. Time after breakfast, after feeding hogs and chickens. Time, and Valena with nothing much to do but sit by her mom, waiting for a tell to rise in her. It was summer, you know, and no school. Well, Valena didn't even know she was waiting. But somehow, if she stayed still near a grown-up in her family, she'd hear something she'd not heard before.

She was sitting on the grass next to her mom's lawn chair. *We don't have a lawn, though,* Valena thought. *Lawns are all over the same green with no mole holes, no crabgrass. Lawns are mostly beyond us on the other side of town. We have lots of crabgrass, and moles that make long rows for themselves to tunnel in. That's why what we have green is only a yard — not a lawn.*

Valena and her mom were resting in the shade under the big maple while clothes dried on the clothesline. Valena's mom's head went back and forth, looking to see what might come or go down the road. She had a dish towel in her hand. She fanned it across herself to keep the flies moving away.

"You are fanning them over on my side," Valena told her.

"I'm just helping them get across me to you. They tell me that's where they are going."

"Ah, Mom!"

Harriet chuckled. Then a car came. Valena recognized it.

"Uncle Rafe," she said. She watched him go by in his dark blue automobile. It was all washed clean and shiny. Valena could see he was in a shirt and tie. His jacket was probably on the seat next to him.

Valena's mom smiled and waved the dish towel as he looked at them. He seemed like a dark shadow in proper clothes. Then he looked on ahead. Valena didn't wave. She just looked back at him. She never said anything to Uncle Rafe. But just then, she happened to think something. Never would've thought it if she hadn't been sitting there with her mom at a certain time of day at the right moment.

Valena's mom said to her, and Valena recalled that she said it every year, "There goes Rafe, on his way to Ripley."

This is the first time I'm right here with her, Valena thought. And this time Valena said right back, "Why does he go there?"

"Because," her mom said. "Ripley, Ohio, is on the Ohio River. Same where your Graw Luke crossed."

Valena sat still a long time, just the way she knew Uncle Rafe would be sitting in his car, with just about only the car moving. It was as if she knew but never remembered hearing it. She knew what her mother was saying, where Graw Luke crossed.

"He goes by himself?" Valena asked, saying it more like she knew it was the truth.

"Who's by himself?" her mom said.

Valena stared at her. She'd meant Uncle Rafe. But she changed it in her head to mean her great-grand-paw, her Graw Luke, what she knew to call him.

"What's going on?" Valena said softly. There were white, fluffy clouds in the sky, and a breeze just above their heads.

"Every year, Rafe goes down to Ripley," Valena's mom said, "where they crossed, and the Rankins gave them transit."

"But why? What?" Valena asked. "They? Who?" She watched Laddie cross the road. Careful of traffic. *Watch out, Laddie.* He seemed to pace a little slower these summer days.

"She was a Cloud," Valena's mom said. "Although Graw Luke used the name Harper."

Valena looked up above. "What?" Fluffy clouds spread out everywhere. *Gonna be a fine day for lazing,* she thought. *Already is.*

"What cloud is that?" Valena asked her mom.

"Proud Mary," her mom said.

Valena laughed at her. Threw back her head and pumped her leg crossed over the other. Thinking, *she's told a joke I can figure out in a little while.* Valena grinned all over her face; she watched the morning grow. Her mom fanned the flies and began. Her voice was as warm and bright as the sunshine on Valena's shirt. Telling about this one particular cloud.

CHAPTER NINE

Proud Mary

The boy should have known from Mary's murmurs. He grew used to the sound — like the wind whistling. She had him by the hand with her long dress bunched in her fingers. At any moment she might throw the wide dress hem over his shoulders, keep him warm. It was springtime, but it was coldtime. It was damptime. All this she would whisper in the air, knowing the sound of her would comfort him. He caught the whispers in his ears.

They walked steadily. He kept his eyes closed at first. But then he would trip and fall to his knees, pulling her down with him. She'd jerk him up. *Don't resist. Don't be afraid,* came in his ears. *Keep your eyes open. You can see in the dark if you look. Feel with your feet and eyes. Keep in time with my feet, as close as you can get to me without stepping on them. Stay close and don't clomp! Stay quiet so we can get gone. We are running. We are going. To Maud Free.*

Once, he started to say something. She jerked him so hard he almost fell. *You say nothing,* he heard in his ears. And then for a long time, nothing came to him, no sound of her. He got so he could be half-asleep on his feet while they moved — on the air, it felt like. All at once, she would squeeze his hand, and they would stop stone-still in the dark. *Heard something,* came in his ears. *Anyhow, almost dawn. Time to lay low.* She would lean always left and scrunch down in a thicket, behind bushes, trees, any wildness that was near. It was forest after all. Forever forest. Lay low forever, it seemed to him.

She would cover him with part of her dress, and he would lean his head on her hip and sleep with his eyes open, seeing dreams. Sometimes, he'd hear her in his ears. Telling about a great day when he reached Maud Free and began to live.

There was something else. He'd almost missed it. Something, the sound of it, in whispers and murmurs, made him feel forsaken. He couldn't understand the words. Are you my mother? He wasn't sure. But once the forlorn feeling circled him, it would leave. And he would fall deeper into dreams where he grew strong in the hard light of Maud Free.

It came to him one rainy night, when they had stopped in a cave. How she knew her way in the dark. How she knew to find the cave. How she knew what tree to hug. She hugged trees all along the way. She felt them until she would whisper softly and go on.

Why do you do that? Never spoken, but it was as if he had. The answer came to his ears. *Moss grows on the north side of trees. We journey north. To Maud Free.* Other times, at vague, first light, she hugged a tree. He was frightened when it hugged her back. Whispers and sighs. What was said he couldn't cipher.

The cave was dry. There were dry clothes. Carefully, the woman examined the clothes in the flame of a small lantern. She gave him something dry to wear. He took off the wet ones and she snapped them straight. Laid them out to dry. Leave them, for the next travelers. She laid out her long dress and sat there in what appeared to be a nightshirt. There were no dry clothes that would fit her.

T'will be dry enough come morning. Her whisper seemed lighter, clearer. Speaking about her long dark dress that had kept both of them warm. She turned it this way and that by the lantern heat.

Exhausted, shivering. He slept as soon as he laid his head down on his arms. She lay beside him, finally, one of her arms across him. It almost covered him, he was that small. But in his sleep, he grew warm enough.

He did not awaken until she lifted her arm off him. It was dull light in the cave. They were not alone. Two more travelers. Women — one old, one, no more than a girl. She had a blistery scar from her temple to her chin. He turned away, not wanting to stare.

The tree that had hugged her, the man, came to the cave. He brought water and bread; then, murmurs between them. He left again.

She and the older woman spoke. Whispers. When would he be old enough to hear everything? But he could understand some of it. Said, "Safe enough to travel by light of day."

"Whomever you meet," the elder woman told them, "say you need to find a doctor for the boy.

He looks sickly. They'll believe you. Ask where the doctor is — you have to find a doctor, s'what you say."

They had no real trouble. They walked a path through trees. It felt to him they were down in a great deep hole. They were walking up and up until his legs ached. Then, they were outside of a little town. Houses, chimney smoke. Chickens. Soon, there came hustle and bustle.

It was all like a road he saw in his dreams. Was it real? It was where all them cooked their meals in the open. There by the road was a black and huge kettle over an open fire. All them ate out of the kettle. Or if they could make bowls, they used them. All them ate together, slept in the same shelter — boys and two men. And got up at first light, and did as they were told. There was another shelter with women and girls.

Was the woman with him one of *them*? Mary. He didn't remember how he knew her name. Was she his mother? Why did he think so, and where had he heard of such a thing? And why not? He didn't know.

Now, the two of them made their way. There were a few houses. One fair-skin woman in a bonnet stopped as they were passing by. It was then he saw that his Mary was tall and stout. It was as if he'd come into the light. Saw that she'd combed her hair; had put on a clean shawl taken from the bundle she carried. She had given him a small blanket to hold around himself. She kept a strong hand on his shoulder. There was misty rain falling on him; he pulled the blanket tightly over his hair.

All around were houses, smells, sounds of living. He'd heard sounds like that on the "hard-ground," the boys had called where all them stayed. Where they did always what they were told and never spoke unless told to speak. But here, sounds, voices, came as they cared to, went when they would. He thought of Maud Free.

Mary spoke up. Her tone was startling, high but soft. "Please, my boy has a fever. Is there a doctor nigh?"

The fair woman stared at them. Moved back a pace, and then another. "Why, yes," she said, finally. "Dr. Patterson. Just keep going straight till straight jogs right. Right around, you'll see the sign. Your boy looks sick." Something made him cough. Some sense of what was going on, a guise, a mask, made him feel a cold coming. He shivered; sneezed.

He and Mary moved then. He looked back. The woman was staring after them. He was afraid.

Don't go that way, he wanted to tell his Mary. *Stay outside. Don't go in.*

She did as she pleased. Around a corner, they saw the apothecary sign. They walked in. No one in the store. Then a man, fair as the fair woman had been, came through a door. Came, looked them up and down.

Mary spoke in her high voice, now loud enough to hear clearly in the air. "A friend told me to come. This boy needs some fixings. Been cold, and caught cold, I spec'."

The man looked her up and down again. She was the taller of the two. The doctor looked at him. Touched his forehead.

"He will catch sickness soon enough," the man said. And then: to the Mary — "Any friend of yours is a friend of mine."

The doctor led them to an inner room. There was a fireplace. There was a table. The boy sat on the floor by the fire. Afraid to lie down, or do anything that might make the fair man angry. But a fair woman came with a pallet. She gestured for him to lie on it; so he did. The firelight made him sleepy. He closed his eyes. He felt so bad. So sick and lonesome.

Someone put food on the table. He could smell its good smell. He sat up. Gently, someone led him to a chair. Food like he'd not had often.

A thick broth with potatoes. Bread with butter. Honey, and he had some. Someone put it on his bread. He had an egg. There was ham with syrup.

Mary . . . his mother? . . . talked with the doctor.

"It's safe here," he told her. "There are many friends. Quakers. You needn't hide anymore." He smiled at her. "We'll find work for you. The boy will do light chores — wood gathering, feeding animals. He'll have his board."

"We'll provide you with day clothes," a fair woman said. "Then, you'll look like any one of you going to market."

His Mary shook her head. "They know I travel with the boy."

"We'll disguise you as a man, if you wish. We'll put a wig on the boy — but you needn't run any farther. You are fairly safe here," he said. "This is the North. I won't lie to you. There are still bounty hunters. But not one of you has been stolen from us in three years."

She simply told him. "I won't stay here. It's not north enough. I go to Maud Free."

"Ahhh," he said. The doctor sighed. "Then you will ride out," he told her. "You will not walk the rest of the way. You have come far enough on your own, Mary. Proud of you!"

"We crossed at Ripley," she told him. "A man with nine sons helped us."

The doctor laughed. "That big John!" he said. "With his lantern high up and his bell ringing."

"Yes! Yes!" she hollered, loud. "I heard the bell, and I thought it was him. We all knew of him; well, I was still scared. But when I saw the lantern, high up on the cliff, I knew it was the signal. I knew it was him."

Words tumbled out of her. "Old boat was leaky. I had Luke fill my hat and empty it over the side. Did that all the way across."

The boy had no memory of it. Until she spoke of it. Now he remembered. Remembered he was Luke.

"Never again," she said, "see so much water."

"The river can be treacherous," said the doctor.

I know it. Said in that murmur again. *Never again. Never go back.* She gasped, frightened all at once. The only time he saw that she had been. He never knew that about her.

"Are you my mother?" For the first time, he spoke.

He saw the man stare at him hard. And move toward the door. He saw Mary's eyes run before she rose, following the doctor.

Soon, she came back with a bottle and a spoon. She gave him spoonfuls from the bottle. It tasted hot and sweet. He made a face. And looked at her. "Are you my mother?"

Sadness swam in her eyes. *I am.* Like a whimper.

He smiled at her and patted her cheek. His hand was lighter than her dark face. She took his hand, then, and held it to her lips.

"Will they whip us? Where we're going?"

"No," she said. "You'll be free." She and the fair woman left the room.

Valena had her eyes closed but opened them when her mom stopped talking. "Is that it?" She was surprised to find herself and her mom still in the yard. She had been so carried away to another time.

Her mom was silent, staring at the clouds. "No, not all," she said, finally. She stood and smoothed her dress.

"Wait!" Valena said. "What else? How do you know what the boy felt, what he said? How do you know he was sick?"

Her mom went on toward the house. "My daddy told me so." Her back to Valena. "Handed down in the family that way. All this time." She walked off into the house.

"But wait!"

"That's all for now," her mom called from

inside the screen. She was inside before Valena could move.

Valena climbed into the lawn chair and folded her hands in her lap. It was hard to come back from there and not know what came next. She wondered if Graw Luke, the boy, and Mary, got where they were going. Were they safe? Did they find Maud Free?

In her mind, the boy still sat in another time where she couldn't reach him. Couldn't help him. There, left with only the food. Alone at the table.

Me. I would've sat with him.

CHAPTER TEN

Freight Train in the Green

"Laddie is acting the fool," Melinda said.

"Oh, be quiet," Valena said. They had stopped way down the Gravel Pit Road. Way beyond where Melinda lived. Way far, about a mile and a half from home. Laddie kept chasing his tail and falling over when he caught it. Acting like he lost his balance. Most of the time, he missed catching his tail. Then, Laddie would stare at them, showing teeth. He was scaring Melinda with his acting up, although she never said so.

"I'm thinking about finding a good cornfield," Valena said. "Get Laddie some good shade, and us, too."

"We leave Laddie outside the corn, beside the road," Melinda pressed. "Guard our bikes."

"Who's going to fool around with our bikes out here?"

"Anybody going by," Melinda said. "See bikes, and take them. Or try to find us in the corn. We could take our bikes in the corn, too."

"You are always thinking bad," Valena told her. "Anyhow, Laddie only guards us. And today, he won't stay still." Valena eyed him. Something was bothering him.

They stopped to rest on their bikes. Fields of corn closed in the road on each side. The high, green corn hung limp. Laddie walked around Valena and Melinda. He paced a short way up the road and back again.

"He's acting real silly," Melinda said.

It's true, Valena thought. Laddie was growling at the air, at nothing.

"Maybe he thinks it's time for him to go meet your dad coming home," Melinda said.

"No, that's not it," Valena said. "I'm thinking the heat's got him. It's so real hot."

"Distemper," Melinda said. "Maybe!"

Valena stared at her cousin, pretending she thought Melinda was silly. But she didn't know what distemper really was.

"Means when animals froth at the mouth and go clear crazy," Melinda explained. "Then they can bite you."

"Maybe some kind of rabies," Valena said, hoping Melinda hadn't heard of it.

Melinda kept quiet.

Laddie headed back down the road toward home. He was growling again. He jumped at something they couldn't see. "I'm following Laddie," Valena said. "I've known him all my life. And he wants us to go home!"

It was a long way back. As they pedaled, heat made pools of water appear in the road. The pools disappeared as they rode up to them.

"Mirages," Valena said. "Dad says it's a trick of seeing. Your eyes see what's not there. Heat does it, I guess. Must be near a hundred out here. Feels like the heat's coming up from the road."

"I know it," Melinda said back. "Oh, but I could drink some water right about now! Laddie's thirsty, too."

Up ahead, Laddie waited for them. His tongue hung out over his side teeth. When they got almost to him, he'd start pacing again.

"I can't breathe," Melinda went on. They biked slowly.

"Feels like it got hotter all of a sudden. Do you smell that?" Valena asked.

"What?"

Valena thought she could taste the air. There was an odor to it. And there were all these funny clouds, darkening the sky. Strange egg shapes poked out of darker gray clouds. Some of the egg shapes appeared to open, and little dark streams hung down from them. "I don't like it up there, looking like that," she said.

"I don't like how everything looks kinda yellow-green," Melinda said.

They rode faster, trying to coast, panting from the heat. Now their arms were sleek with sweat.

Suddenly, there was a puff of wind, stirring the corn, and it began raining on them. Only it turned out not to be rain. It felt like sleet in the wintertime, only harder. Real cold, little seeds all in their hair.

Laddie practically had his nose to the ground, growling. The hair on his neck stood on end. He shook it out a minute. Came back to Valena and nipped at her heels. "Stop it!" she yelled at him.

He growled, snapping at her, hurrying her along. They reached Melinda's house first. They dropped their bikes in the yard and ran for the door.

Melinda pounded, but it was locked. Running around to the back, the back door was locked. "Where'd Mama go? Mama? Mama!" Nobody came.

"Come home with me!" Valena was already back on her bike.

Laddie barked like crazy at them. The rain seeds were bigger. It was hailing.

They raced through the sound, like wind rushing through winter wheat. Through the hits on their heads and skin.

"It hurts!" Melinda started crying.

What is happening? Not far, Valena thought. *Don't cry, girl! Let's get home.*

They rounded the corner. They saw Babysis. Coming out of the house, looking, shielding her head with her arms, Babysis had seen them. She started jumping up and down, motioning them home.

Valena hollered, half-crying, "Babysis! Mom!" The egg clouds were so low and misty, and looking like something inside them wanted to bust out.

They hopped off their bikes and threw themselves into Babysis's arms. Babysis said, "Didn't you know? There's a bad storm coming."

"Nooo! We didn't!" they moaned. There hadn't been any warning, except for Laddie and the clouds.

Babysis shielded them inside. She and Valena's mom directed them to the cellar. "Hurry," Harriet said, her voice calm but serious.

CHAPTER ELEVEN

Time to Hold Tight

It wasn't much of a place. There were wood steps going down into darkness. On the bottom cellar step, a musty odor of damp earth hit them. The cellar was only half dug out, with a dirt floor. The other half of it, on the far side of the house, was only a crawl space. The dug-out part was deep below the house's foundation. On all sides were shelves holding her mom's canned pre-serves — peaches, cherries, apple jam, green beans, tomatoes. Oh, so many kinds of good stuff to eat in the cold winter months. Harriet flicked on a light.

"I don't like it down here much," Valena said.

"It's what we have to save us," Babysis said.

Valena didn't have time to ask from what. The hail was hammering now.

All of a sudden, they heard a racket from above. Sounding like thunder. Like feet, stomping. The cellar door burst open. Adam flew through, leaping down the steps, slamming the door behind him. The force rattled the shelves of preserves on either side.

"Where were you?" their mom asked. "Slow down, or you'll knock over my canning!"

"Oooh, yeah," he said, tiptoeing. "Oooh!" Rubbing his arms. "That hail nearly knocked me down! I was clear downtown. I heard the twelve o'clock noon siren go off; only, it was two o'clock instead of twelve. And I knew it was bad news."

"Uncle Dell and them weren't home!" Valena said. "They locked up the house, too."

"They must be out of town on special shoppings," their mom said.

All at once, Valena leaped up. "Laddie! Laddie! I forgot Laddie!"

She was up the steps when Adam grabbed her. "No!" He held on to her. "You can't go up."

"Laddie'll get hailed! I left him out there!" Valena cried.

"Hush!" her mom said.

"He'll squeeze under the back porch," Adam said.

She imagined it, a freight train, going fast, cutting through the green air. It all made her feel really funny. Her ears popped.

"Cyclone!" Adam said.

"Tornado!" Babysis whispered loud. "Oh, we're gonna get it."

"Hush," Harriet said. "We're getting the hail. It means the twister is someplace else. Poor souls! They say that when there's hail, you are in the tail of it."

Valena realized her mom had to shout to be heard.

They huddled together, up against the dark, southwest wall of the cellar. A strange cold-and-hot air flowed on the dampness around them.

They waited and wondered about the storm. Valena's dad was there on her mind now. Laddie, fleetingly. She couldn't think long about anything, for listening to the hard roar. It wasn't like anything else. It made them all shiver.

"He'll crawl up against the foundation."

"Listen to the wind!" Babysis said. She grabbed hold of Valena.

They all listened. They could feel the wind hit the house. It whistled and whammed, strumming a steady low note. "Whummmm." The hail roared. The house shook.

Valena and Melinda clung to each other. Babysis held both of them close. Harriet took hold of Adam's arm. "Mom, it's going to be okay," he said. She leaned on him and closed her eyes.

We could be out there, Valena thought. *Oh, Laddie; sorry, Laddie!* A sob caught in her throat.

The hail sound drowned out everything else. Huge hailstones, come alive enough to roar like lions.

Something crashed down outside. They stayed still. Harriet's canned peaches popped their lids. So did the green beans, spilling down the steps.

They heard a loud, rushing sound, like a train. It was going around the countryside, Valena could tell.

Valena cried out inside: *Dad! Daddy?*

But they all stayed quiet; before long, the storm eased off. The hail was slowing.

The freight train had come really close. Every now and again they could hear sirens around the outskirts, in other towns. Thin sounds, like quick, painful cuts in the air.

It came down from the egg clouds and green of the sky. The twister train! Valena thought.

"We never saw this coming," Harriet said. "It must've come up so fast, out of the southwest."

"Must've," Adam agreed.

"We saw that the sky was just awful," Melinda said. "It had egg clouds."

"It sure did!" Babysis said. "I looked out from upstairs, and everything was this funny color."

"Green," Valena said. "Laddie acted crazy — Laddie!" She began to whimper.

"Take it easy," Adam told her. "We'll find him. Don't you worry."

Adam opened the cellar door. He looked around. "We're still here! House!" Cooling fresh air enveloped them. Adam grinned. "Yeah!"

Valena came up and held his hand.

"My windows! Screens! All the windows were up," her mom said.

"I'll help you mop up the rain," Babysis told her. For rain had come through the screens and wet the floors.

"Let's find Laddie!" Valena said to Adam.

They went outside to look. "I have to go find Tonya . . ." he left off.

"You love her?" Valena asked, before she thought. *How could I have said that now?* she wondered.

Adam walked off from her. She pouted. "I just asked. I didn't mean anything!"

"Oh, my!" Babysis said. She stood in the door-way. "Look at the ground!"

The ground was covered — winter snow. No, rock-sized hail, glistening in sunlight. There were clear patches of blue sky. The sun was shining through. No more funny-looking clouds, either. Just rain-looking clouds, high up. And thunder, off in the distance.

A large tree limb had fallen across the road.

"Goodness sakes!" their mom exclaimed. "I bet my clothesline . . . my chickens!"

"In the chicken house," Adam called from the back yard. "The clothesline is down. I can fix it back up. The chicken house is leaning some."

Valena was around to the back of the house

after Adam, with Melinda right behind them. Just then, Laddie came crawling out from under the wood porch.

"Laddie, boy!" Adam said. Laddie was practically smiling at them. "You okay?" Adam asked him. Laddie made a whimpering sound. He was wet and shivery and all-over muddy. He walked all trembly and stiff-legged over to Adam. But his tail was wagging. "Hey, boy!" Adam said gently.

Adam looked relieved. He held Laddie's face in his hands. "Can't hardly pet you, you're so muddy."

Valena came up beside him. "Is Laddie sick?" she asked. "He acts like it."

"Nothing wrong with him — is there, boy? We need to try to dry him some."

Laddie acted kind of weary. Valena ran inside for some old towels and ran back; she and Melinda wiped him down. When they finished, they let him lie there in the sun with the towels over him.

Valena petted him through the towels.

"He'll sleep in the kitchen tonight," Adam said. "And get a bath tomorrow." Adam got to his feet, wiping his wet hands on his jeans.

Laddie lay that way, stretching and then sleeping.

"Acting all right now," Valena said. "But before, on the road under those clouds. Oh, brother, Laddie was something else!"

"Like he was fighting the air," Melinda said.

"Probably felt the storm coming," Adam told her.

"Look at the roof, Adam. How is it?" their mom asked. She stood there on the back porch, just looking over everything.

"Hard to say." Adam shielded his eyes to see better. "Dad'll have to get somebody who knows what hail can do."

Then, there was silence. Valena knew why. Probably their dad was still at work in town. No one said anything about him. They knew that when Adam went out, he would look to find him. Still, it was a worry.

A little while later, their mom said, "Adam, I tried to phone, but there's no sound on the line." Adam left then, in a trot. He would locate their dad and Tonya, too. Why he shunned a bike, Valena would never know. Well, he was a runner, and runners were strange!

Their mom, Babysis, Valena, and even Melinda would be restless until they found out everybody was okay.

Valena's mom looked sharply at Melinda, then at Valena. They came up to her on the porch. She studied their mood, put a hand over Melinda's hair. "They'll be home soon," she said. "Not to worry."

"It's all right, they'll be here," Melinda said. Then Melinda stood tall, just the way Valena would've tried to if it had been both her folks missing.

The air was warmer now, like placid summer

air. The ice on the ground was thick and cold. But it was melting fast. Valena began to play with it. Melinda joined in. They threw the ice stones. Laddie leaped up, suddenly wide awake, trying to catch hailstones in his mouth. "Look at Laddie!" Valena cried. "You good dog! Catch it, boy!"

"Watch it. You'll hurt him in the mouth," Babysis warned.

Laughing, Valena and Melinda turned to throw iceballs at the big old maple.

Their dad came home early, finally. They all had a million questions. "Were you out in it — we were, me and Melinda. Did you worry?"

"Yes, I worried! I wasn't in it."

"We all went to the basement."

Laddie lowered his head, as if he'd done something wrong. Then he came slowly forward, to be petted.

"Laddie, how are you? Did you bring the girls home?"

"He did!" Valena said. "How'd you know?"

"That's his job," her dad said. He had an embrace for Valena and Melinda. A kiss on Harriet's forehead and cheek. He saw Melinda's face twitching with nerves and said, "Your mom and dad and sister will be around any minute, I'm sure."

They could see she held back tears. "Honey, they're fine," Harriet said soothingly. "Don't you worry about a thing."

Valena told about how she and Melinda had been far from home and how strange Laddie had acted.

"Well, it's all over now," her dad said. "It was a bad storm, though. I'll have to have our roof checked."

"They say it hit mostly barns and such. But they say it about shaved one corner of the county seat."

Her dad hadn't named the county seat, but Valena knew its name and where it was. In the

County Building, all their names and birth cer-
tificates and more such like that were kept.
Valena knew that if Melinda's folks had gone special shopping, they'd gone to the county seat
town. Seven miles from where they lived. It had
big new stores in a row near their fairgrounds.

Maybe they've been grazed by the tornado,
Valena thought. Uncle Dell would know what to
do, know how to hide from a storm. And Aunt
Demmie would tell Cynthia, Melinda's big sister,
not to be afraid. The bad weather could have hurt
them, but more than likely, it missed them. *Lottsa
other folks it could run into, 'stead of them*, Valena
thought. But that would be bad, too.

Melinda all at once let go; couldn't hold back
anymore. She sobbed softly, just as if she'd heard
what Valena was thinking.

They were inside sitting down, waiting, although no one had said. Valena's dad was in the
big armchair. Her mom sat on a straight chair.
Babysis sat on the arm of her dad's chair. And

Valena and Melinda were as close as they could be on the couch.

Every now and again, someone would make small talk.

"Did you see Adam?"

"Yes," her dad said. "Ran into him with Tonya."

"Ah, he was looking for her."

Melinda sucked in her breath. They were all silent then. And they stayed there, sitting for another hour.

Valena's mom and dad went out in the kitchen to see to supper. Exhausted and scared, Melinda fell asleep on Valena's shoulder. She had her hand in Valena's. Valena took a deep breath, feeling sad and afraid herself. If something had happened to Uncle Dell and them, she didn't know what they'd all do.

Maybe Melinda will come live with us, she thought. *Well, that'll have to be the way. But . . .* She fell asleep before she could finish thinking.

Later, the two woke up. Supper wasn't quite ready. They could tell, because Valena's mom hadn't come to wake them. They went out, carefully seating themselves on the front steps. They were quiet mostly, being polite, trying not to talk about what was scary. They noticed that all the ice had melted.

There were trees down all over town, Adam told, when he came back with Tonya. Tonya hugged them before she went inside. She didn't stay long. It was like, everybody wanted to be home with their families. Like, you couldn't tell what would happen next. There were reports of more storms.

I hate to see the night come, Valena thought. *It's going to be dark soon. Scary, Nightly, Nightly.*

They heard a rattletrap car coming. Didn't lift their heads up from their arms on their knees. Until it turned into Valena's gravel driveway.

Black car, covered with dents and smashed in

on the driver's side. The driver kicked the car door a couple of times, and it creaked open. Slowly the cousins stood.

"Daddy!"

"Uncle Dell!"

It was him, all right.

Melinda flew into his arms.

Valena ran up the steps. "Dad! Mom! It's Uncle Dell! It's Uncle Dell!"

Everybody emptied from the house. "Wellll!" came from Valena's dad. "Glad to see you!" With a firm hug, he gave his brother space to tell.

"It was something!" Uncle Dell said. They waited, nodded at him, patting his arms and shoulders. "It was the hail that destroyed the car." He glanced back at his dented and wrecked car. The top was all smashed. "Not just our automobile, but up and down Main Street. Every car! Well, but the wind about killed us, turned us over and then back again. I tell ya. Nothing like a tornado! Whoom!"

They waited. "Demmie's okay," he said, and sighed, his voice shaking.

"Oh, I'm so glad!" Harriet said.

"She's at the hospital with Cynthia."

They hushed and held their breaths. "Demmie's got a mild concussion, and Cynthia got her arm and elbow broken somehow. She came out of the car as it turned over, we think. But we were on the ground, so she didn't have to fall far." He coughed, cleared his throat. "It was bad, I tell ya. You couldn't see anything for all the dust and stuff in the air. And then, you could see stuff flying at you. We were ducking, and we flipped in the air. God-awful day, I tell ya."

They waited. Harriet took him by the arm, patted it. Uncle Dell winced. Melinda whimpered. Valena's dad shook his head. They all stood there. Uncle Dell sighed. "I guess I got some bruises. You don't feel stuff like that until later. Demmie can't stop shaking. I have to go back to the hospital."

"Have something to eat first," Harriet said.

Uncle Dell stared at the ground. "I want to sit down a minute." They helped him inside. He walked as if his legs were made of cement. Melinda was crying now.

She sat with her father while he ate. He didn't talk again until he had Harriet's coffee and a piece of yellow cake with chocolate icing. "I tell ya," he said again. He shook his head about the storm and said, "Harriet, I needed that."

"Well," Valena's mom said. "Help yourself to more."

"I had plenty."

Then he concentrated on Melinda, put his arm around her. "You all right, baby-girl?"

Her mouth was quivering as she spoke. "Me and Valena were riding our bikes. Laddie knew something was wrong. He made us go home."

"That old dog is something else!" Uncle Dell exclaimed.

"But nobody was home," Melinda whimpered. "You all went off and left me."

"Now. No, we didn't."

"The house was locked," Valena said as kindly as she could. But she was mad about that, for both Melinda's sake and her own. The house should've stayed open for them.

"We couldn't get in," Melinda told her dad. "We had to race over to Valena's. The hail hurt us, too!"

"That storm cellar door stays unlocked," Uncle Dell said. "Why didn't you go in there? I always leave it open for just in case."

The two of them were silent. "I forgot," Melinda said finally.

"So did I," Valena said. "We . . . just were scared half to death."

"Well," he said, "this time we were lucky. But remember that cellar, anytime, just in case. You go there first if you are over that way and scared. Understand?"

"Yes," they both said.

And he told Melinda, "We went without you because your birthday's coming. Well, it was all innocent. Whoever thought a storm like that . . . We would've been back in an hour or two. We knew you would be with your cousin." He looked at the two of them. He took Melinda's face in his hand. "Not mad at me?"

"No, Daddy."

"All right, then. Everything's going to be all right."

"Will Cynthia, will Mom be okay?" And Melinda began to sob again.

"Of course they will, don't you think about it," Uncle Dell said. "Not to worry. They hurt some now, but they'll be fine." He folded her close. "You don't know how lucky we were."

Later, before he left, he asked Harriet if Melinda could spend the night with them. He had to get his truck and go back to the hospital. See if Demmie and Cynthia could be released.

"They weren't hurt over-bad, considering," he said. "We were lucky, again! I feel the bruises all over!" He grinned a sad kind of twitching smile. "I was there when they brought in the *real* hurt and dying." He shook his head. "It was just the saddest sight.

"Tornadoes," he went on. "You should see that town. Like somebody sliced it off on one side. It got the courthouse clock. Believe that? And it got both sides of Main Street coming into town. Houses, just gone."

Melinda started to cry again. "You sure Mommy's alive?"

"Oh, honey," he said. "I'm sorry. Your mother hit her head, but she's all right. You'll see tomorrow. She'll be fine. Now let me go. You stay with Aunt Harriet and Valena."

"Okay," Melinda said. She wanted to go with him, Valena could tell. And she sniffled about it.

"You'll stay with us. There's ice cream and cake. Dinner! We haven't even eaten anything!" Valena told her.

"That's right!" Melinda said. "Haven't eaten anything!"

Valena's dad offered to go with Uncle Dell, but Dell wouldn't have it. He didn't know how long he'd be. Might have to stay the night. "I'll be okay," he said, and left. Proud. Valena's dad saw him out.

The girls fixed their plates right from the stove. So did Valena's dad, with Harriet standing over them. "So you don't miss something." She laughed. "Don't miss my green beans!"

"We won't, Mom."

After that, everything seemed to get normal. Only it got hot outside again. They looked out, watched the clouds and sky as darkness came. There was heat lightning way off, like a searchlight on the horizon.

The girls went up to bed about 9:30. They went sound asleep and didn't hear the wind and storm in the night. Lightning was bright daylight. Valena's mom and dad stayed downstairs, listening to the thunder. Listening for sirens. They heard none. They fell asleep on the couch. Babysis was curled up in the armchair. All of them in the living room slept on and on. Until sunlight streamed through the curtains.

CHAPTER TWELVE

Things Change

There were times when Valena had to say, "I can tell this won't be a good day." She didn't always know what she meant by it. But it happened that way.

There was one such day when you couldn't see a cloud. There was an all-over dazzle, like somebody up there forgot to wash the windows. But the sun got through anyhow. And the glaring light burned, and could make you squint your eyes.

This day, none of them had a thing to do. So

Adam got his baseball and catcher's mitt, and everybody played, even Harriet. Even Laddie, when they could get him to catch the ball.

Melinda was up to bat. Babysis was behind the plate. Adam was pitching, and Valena was out toward the road to catch fly balls. Only she would usually daydream. She found baseball so boring and usually forgot to catch the ball. Laddie was right behind her. Why'd he have to be there?

Adam threw the ball. "Hit it, Melinda!"

She swung. Valena backpedaled to catch a fly ball, in case it came to her. Laddie was too close, and she fell backwards on top of him.

Melinda missed the ball. But her swinging bat caught Babysis right in the eye, with all the force of a good strike. It knocked Babysis down to her knees.

Everybody started screaming and jumping up and down. But it was Valena who ran up first, to see Babysis on the ground, holding her hand over her eye. Babysis's eye must've come out from the blow. *Babysis, with one eye!* Valena's stomach turned over.

Harriet heard the screams and came running. She saw Babysis holding her face, and she pulled her to her feet.

"Oh, my God," she said. "Oh, Lord! Take your hand away. Please, Baby, let me see . . ."

When she saw, they all saw. Melinda stood there, still with the bat at her feet. Her face was twisted in fear. She couldn't even cry. Her mouth pulled back from her teeth, and her eyes were like slits.

Valena shivered. Everybody stopped screaming, except Babysis. It was just awful. Her eye wasn't out on her face, the way Valena was sure it would be, at first. But it had swollen to twice its size in seconds — bleeding and swollen closed. Her mom took Babysis into the house. She said nothing to anyone else.

Melinda fell to the ground with her arms covering her head. Adam sat on the step, holding his ears. "I had to start it! Get my bat and ball," he kept saying, over and over. "Stupid! I had to start it!"

Valena just stood there. Laddie walked from Melinda to Adam and back to Valena, trying to comfort.

It was just one of those bad times. Babysis went to the doctor and got her eye wound sterilized and bandaged. At home, she cried a lot from the purple bruise all around and the swelling. Said it felt like a basketball. Valena sat there and watched over her, right beside her on the couch. Once or twice Babysis held her sister's hand. Valena told her, "Melinda's really sorry. So is Adam."

"I know she didn't mean it," Babysis said. "It just happened. Oh, but it hurts!"

Adam came in once or twice. "Hey, Babysis. You can knock me in the head if you want to."

That made her almost smile. "I don't want to," she said kindly.

"You can have my supper for a week."

She smiled. "I'll take it."

That made him feel better. Then Babysis moaned and cried.

As Babysis slowly got better, the dog days came. Day after day, there came dry winds in straight lines.

You never can tell about those winds coming, Valena thought. They came low to the ground, without a whistle or warning. They could knock down fences and sheds, and blow hot dust in your face.

It was a kind of pouting, moping, dark time for her. The wind stayed hot. Melinda went to camp. "Get her mind off hurting Babysis," Aunt Demmie said.

Valena felt best being home in her own yard. It was the first summer the two cousins weren't together all of the time. She didn't want company. She became annoying, trailing her mom. She, with Laddie, nearly caused a wreck in the kitchen, in the dining room, or even the living room, trying to help her mom straighten the house.

"Valena, why don't you and Laddie go outside?"

"We're your helpers," Valena said. But she knew they weren't. "Besides, it's windy and too hot out."

"Well, you're underfoot," her mom said.

"You don't want me around!" Valena began to sob. She felt so awful.

"Child, what's gotten into you?" Harriet stopped what she was doing to hug Valena to her. Laddie came up and leaned against Harriet. "I swear, Laddie, if you don't stop it. You act like a second child," Harriet scolded.

"Nobody cares about me!" Valena cried.

"My goodness, what's got into you today? What's upset you?"

Valena leaned into her mom, feeling the warm

safety of her. "Don't make me go back to school," she whined. "I can't stand it. Can I stay home, and you teach me?" She sobbed.

"Well, I never! School's almost a whole month away. And you love school."

"I do *not love it*," Valena cried. "Let it stay away from me, too. I don't want to go to sixth grade."

"Why, for heaven's sake! Sixth grade is in the new middle school. You'll love it," her mom said.

"I will not. It'll be pukey, and I don't want it!"

"Valena, you'll have to go."

"I'm not going, and no one can make me."

Sunday rolled around, still hot and dry July; but almost the end of it. Something was troubling behind Valena's eyes. She was headachey, and her mom gave her an aspirin before they went to church. "It's a special day," her mom said.

"I know, I know!" Valena said fretfully. The whole family was going to church because Valena's dad was giving a program where he played his mandolin, and everybody listened. There wasn't another classical mandolin player in town that she knew of.

The church was packed, every seat taken. Valena and her mom sat in the first-row pew. Adam and Tonya sat in the back. Like his dad, Adam couldn't stand crowds much.

When her dad played his music, Valena went off in a world of just her and her dad. The tinkling sound of it came from her dad's fingers; she knew it was deep within him as well. It took her to a place of calm inside herself. Made her feel like singing quiet songs; maybe someday, play his mandolin. *Wouldn't that be something?* she thought.

She was so proud to be her dad's daughter. She looked around at folks looking at him. Saw their faces full of wonder. They all clapped after each of his pieces. To show they knew how tough a mandolin was to play, and how good he was. He played a long, sweet time. When it was over, the whole congregation stood and applauded. Her dad grinned and held up his hand to them, in thanks, and maybe to make them stop applauding. Valena couldn't tell which. Then, she couldn't wait to shake his hand the way everybody else was doing on the way out.

Home with your family. That was the custom of the churchgoers. At home, Valena's house was easy, the way it could be after church. They all sat around in their Sunday clothes until it was time to eat an early supper around three. Her mom told her dad how much she loved his concert.

"Oh, well," her dad said. He was made uncomfortable by compliments.

Sundays were always special. Then it came time to change into more everyday clothes. Valena put on shorts and a T-shirt. All the windows were open. Flies covered the screens, trying to get in. *It's like somebody shook out a pepper jar,* Valena thought. Maybe it would rain. Flies did that when it was going to. She felt glum again.

She and Adam read the Sunday funnies, the comics. "Go up and make your bed, Valena," her mom said. "Pick up your clothes. You, too, Adam. Your room is messier than your sisters'."

When their mom left them, they both slid behind the couch to hide. Didn't fancy doing anything but what they wanted to do. It was part of what made Sunday special. Valena had scrambled to hide like that since she was way little, following Adam. But this time, their mom was right behind them — with the broom! "Who do you think you're kidding?" She jabbed them with the prickly broom straws.

"Owwww!" they hollered. How'd she find them?

Adam's feet stuck out too far. That's how she finally caught him. Not Valena. She scrunched up even smaller.

Adam went upstairs, arguing all the way.

"Adam, I can hear you! You stay out of the attic," Harriet called.

"But there's good stuff to see up here. Old stuff!" came the muffled reply.

"Adam, you come down from . . ."

Harriet never got the chance to finish. There was a terrible noise, the loudest crunch-and-cracking, splitting-and-breaking sound. Adam exploded down through the ceiling of the living room in a cloud of plaster dust. A foggy haze settled around him. He looked to be snow-covered on a triangle board of attic and floor.

Valena peeked from behind the couch. "Oh, no!" Adam with white eyebrows and white hair. A jagged section of wallpapered ceiling was under him. He'd broken through the attic, the upstairs floor, and through the living room ceiling.

Well, it was an old house!

Adam sat there like a statue, his arms held high. And sneezed. Valena froze into a ball, one eye peeking.

Harriet was right there, with Babysis at her heels. Babysis covered her mouth to keep from laughing. Was it funny? It was funny. But peeking Valena was struck dumb by the sight of her brother.

"Oh, Adam! Wait until your dad . . ." Her mom didn't finish.

Suddenly, Adam, like a streak, was out the front door.

"Adam!" their mom called. "You come right back here and clean up this mess! Wait until your dad sees this!"

But he was gone. He went so fast he left the screen door wide open. A cloud of flies poured in.

Her mom and Babysis stood at the door, trying to see where he'd gone. They said he wasn't in sight anywhere. *Disappeared!* Valena thought. *Whoa, goodness!*

She was caught, then, by Harriet. "Get up from there. You're as bad as your brother."

Glum again, Valena went upstairs and finished her side of the bedroom she shared with Babysis. Then she went outside, to her favorite spot on the front porch. It was shady this time of day. A good place to sit and think and let the time pass.

Boy, she thought. *That was sure something.* And said aloud, as if she were telling Melinda, "Adam hasn't come home. He's been gone since after church almost. Wonder where he went?" She shook her head. "He's not anywhere. No-body's seen him." Whispering it as if to a hidden friend.

Hope he doesn't hop a train to Chicago. What a misshapen summer! I should've gone to camp. Valena sighed.

Adam went into hiding. Babysis had gone over to Tonya's. Maybe Adam was hiding over there.

The sun was going down. Valena could feel a wind just above her head. But the trees were calm at their tops. And Laddie, laying low him-self, was out in the yard. The breeze ruffled the hair on his back. He pricked up his ears. Laddie sat up, listening. And got up, to come to her.

"You want to be petted," Valena said. She obliged him. He leaned close. She hugged him. "Good Laddie. I love you. Good boy."

Laddie backed up a few paces and turned away. He walked across the yard. Going to lie down, rest again. He did that a lot these days. Was it just the heat? She wished it would let go. Dry July. Maybe by the end of the month it would rain, nice and cool. Just a steady rain all night. And in the morning, there would be sunshine on wet grass. That'd be nice!

Laddie walked out of the yard. "Oh," Valena said aloud. *He's going to get Dad. He can hear him from this far! Amazing Laddie! Circus dog! Ha-ha! He'll go to the Point and sit and wait for Dad.* She easily imagined him sitting there.

He sees Dad, and then he'll cross over to the other side and trot on down to meet him. They'll walk home like always, talking and ruffing all the way.

She could see it all. Both of them, talking over

that Sunday. "*Should-a heard me play on the mandolin, Laddie. The folks liked it!*"

"*Ruff! Ruuuff!*"

She forgot about them, in her thoughts of being by herself. She thought, *I like it and I hate it. Why didn't I want to go to camp with Melinda? Well, what if I'm there, and she gets prissy in some clique of girls and leaves me be? She makes me so mad. We've always been together, every single day, every summer. Now, she's gone; she wanted to go, too. And left me alone. Well, shoot! I just wanted to stay close. Be with my folks. My dog. Stay home and be safe.*

Still, things kept on changing.

CHAPTER THIRTEEN

The End Is the Beginning

She never dreamed such harm would come. When it did, gloom and hurt came over Valena in waves. And left her feeling like a damp rag, wrinkled and crimped.

After it happened, evenings, the sun going down, made her hide in her room. Pillows covering her head. She shivered from the slashing sunlight. The only shadowy place she could find was under her bed. Somebody, usually Adam, had to lift the bed and move it out from the wall. Then Babysis and her mom dragged her out.

Valena tossed and turned at night. She had bad dreams. Gargantua came with his wife. Laddie wasn't there when she called for him to save her.

She couldn't even cry anymore. She couldn't stand Babysis coming in and patting her back. "Go away," she'd say. Or, "Babysis! Stop, don't touch me."

Yes, there were some fun times. Telling of Adam, falling through the ceiling. Babysis, her mom, and even Adam, telling it over and over to cousins, family, so many times it became like a cartoon or a comic. There were all these parts to the story. Adam, looking addled: "I swear, I was just standing there. And the floor went out from under me."

Everybody, all the cousins, Uncle Dell and them, liked to hear about it. It took their minds off the . . . other.

Adam, out there. And coming in when he

heard what happened. They even told that. Adam told it. How all thoughts of his getting punished, hiding, paled when he heard they took Laddie away in the man's car.

Man who hit "a dog."

The day it happened, Valena was sitting in a lawn chair next to her mom's. "Don't sit on the ground," her mom had told her. "It's damp with so much rain."

Valena had wanted rain. Screamed for rain in her sleep, after they brought Laddie back, and he lay so still, with a blanket around him, on the kitchen floor. It had started raining that July night.

Melinda said Laddie's eyes were half open, and his tongue was outside of his mouth.

Valena screamed at her: "Stop talking! Stop it! Go back to camp!"

Adam had stayed with Laddie all night. Never left his side. Feeding Laddie water from a turkey baster and giving him bits of food. Which Laddie refused to swallow. Adam had to clean out his mouth a couple of times.

Valena didn't want to know. And she wanted to know, all at the same time.

What happened — Laddie wasn't as fast as he once was, Adam said. Laddie thought he could beat the car. Or maybe he didn't think. But everybody told about it — Babysis, who heard it from their dad. And even Melinda told it, and she was nowhere near there, being still at camp at the time.

"Don't talk! Don't talk about it!" Valena would holler at everybody. And run up the stairs.

No one could console her. She was cold all the time, so that's why she and her mom sat in the sun now, instead of under the old maple.

Finally, she let her mom tell her how it all had come about that evening, when Laddie crossed the road too late. It was the very same early evening when she'd been sitting on the step feeling lonely. She'd hugged Laddie and said she loved him. He walked out of the yard.

Soon after, the car hit him and pitched him through the air. Her dad had seen it all, because Laddie never moved from the Point until he saw her dad coming — her dad's white shirt shining in the waning light.

Dog began to move then. So happy to see his old friend, Man. Both old friends, Dog and Man, happy to see each other. But her dad said he went cold when he saw the car. He raised his hand, trying to get Laddie to turn. He began to run toward him, shouting, "Laddie, no! Go back!"

"But what good would that have done?" her dad said, later. "The driver never saw Laddie."

Driver saw the man raise his hand. Thought maybe the man was flagging him down, needed something. The driver was trying to make up his mind whether he should stop. He decided he would slow, roll down his window when he neared the man. He kept coming.

And heard the hit. Saw this hairy bunch of something, flying through the air. Well, it was that dangerous twilight time. Dusk. Nightly, Nightly! When objects blend and vanish.

"Thought it was — I don't know what — a child, I guess. Scared me to death!" the man had said. "But I saw it was only a dog."

And her dad, bitterly chastising the man. "Just *only* a dog?" Her dad, taking off his jacket and wrapping Laddie in it. And the man, saying he was sorry. He had a pet, he knew how it was. "A *pet*?" said her dad. The man kindly offered to take them to the vet. Both the man and her dad, lifting Laddie gently onto the back seat.

There wasn't much to be done. It was a hard, deadly hit. Adam, when he heard, walked out of a cornfield where he'd fallen asleep and never left Laddie's side. All night in the kitchen on the floor with Laddie.

And woke up the next day. Her mom found

Adam petting Laddie. Leaning over him and petting, and picking pieces of tar road out of his hair.

"Oh!" she'd said. Coming into the kitchen and standing there. Because all at once she knew.

"He's not breathing," Adam said, tears streaming down his face. "What are we to do now?" he whispered.

His dad came in, and the two of them wrapped Laddie in the blanket and took him out to the far corner of the property. Where they put Laddie down.

They stood over the mound of fresh field soil a long time. And then they packed it tight. Her mom and Babysis hadn't come out until the next day.

Later, Melinda had told Valena. And she, Melinda, never even anywhere near.

"So," her mom said now. Like *so* was a beginning all around, Valena thought. Like *so* was final, like the last of the day. *So* put an end to things; stood things on end. "So. Things happen, things change," her mom went on. That's the way it was. They buried him. "We'll remember Laddie," her mom said, "the way we do all that we love."

Valena had her head on the arm of her mom's chair — her face under her mom's hand, which played with strands of her hair.

"Everything changes, you must know that," her mom told her.

"I know it," Valena said. "I don't like it much, either."

"Well," her mom said, like it was a question that had no answer. "We can have another dog."

"No." *There's no other one like Laddie*, Valena was thinking.

When things changed, you let them stay changed. Melinda was back from camp. But Valena didn't want her around because she just didn't. She didn't want to ride her bike because Laddie wouldn't be by her side. She didn't want anything new. She couldn't stop new or change from coming, she guessed, but she sure didn't have to like it.

Sitting there, getting cramped from her position in the lawn chair, she raised her head and sat back. Took her mom by the hand.

"I don't want you to cry anymore," her mom told her.

Valena couldn't talk or she would cry. *Did you tell Adam not to cry anymore?* was what she was thinking. Thinking mean all the time. She couldn't help herself. She just felt so bad.

And looked at the clouds to soothe her mind. Her mouth turned down. She could feel it. Sky, to make things clear to her.

Her mom looked up at clouds and sky. When Valena leaned around, she could see sky and clouds in her mom's eyes. Blue sky and fluffy clouds. Valena's face went to pieces as she said, "Tell about that little boy. He's all alone!"

"Shhh! Don't you cry," her mom cautioned.

Then, a long pause before her mom said, "You mean, your Graw Luke? You never knew him, of course," she said. "But the boy grew up to be your Graw Luke."

"My great-grandpa, all by himself. Proud Mary." Valena managed to speak without crying.

Her mom smiled dimly. "The beginning," she said.

"So," Valena said, and thought — *He never knew me, either.*

Her mom began.

CHAPTER FOURTEEN

Maud Free

He guessed anything was better than walking.

They were in some kind of buggy that had a top on it. It was driven by two horses. The driver was a woman, very small, in men's clothes. He and Mary needn't hide now, the woman said.

"Are you Maud Free?" he asked. And the woman smiled.

Mary smiled. Then they laughed at him. "Maud Free," the woman said. "Not no woman."

"Well," Mary said, "she was, once."

The woman looked at her and smiled, nodded.

Looked at Luke. "Was, once." And laughed. Shook her head. "Not no more."

The woman, Lettie, drove the horses. They rode and they rode. He and Mary had a blanket over them up to their shoulders. The buggy's to-and-fro soon put him to sleep. All he saw when he yawned and woke were trees, woods. Occasionally there were houses.

"Freedom coming yet?" he asked.

Mary uh-huhed him. "It all around us," she told him.

But all he could see were trees and dappled light. Once in a while, smoke in chimneys. Smoke reminded him.

"I thought we was to see a war around," he said.

Mary's eyes were closed. She spoke again, in her whisper, in his ear — she was that close to him. Head turned to his face. "Left war behind us. Uh-huh! Behind time." She chuckled and then was serious. "War over too soon."

"Then why we have to go so far?"

"War over, but the folks who make it, still around us. We don't hide no more. But we ain't to Maud Free yet."

"Huh," was all he could think to say. It was hard to figure. So he took some bread out of the bag she carried. Mary said he could have bread when he wanted. He was lulled to sleep once, after the woman got fresh horses; stopped along the way. Soon after they came to this place.

He awoke to the smell of bacon. Good food smells. He looked out, and all he saw were — "What they call them things? Long wooden things — call it . . ." He couldn't think. Then, he could. "Goods wagons. Called box wagons. Boxcars. That's what it is."

Train wagons, some called them, lined up by twos. He was so busy looking out he didn't realize, at first. Then, he looked beside him. Mary was outside. He looked in front of him at Lettie.

She was standing on the ground, with her

hand up to him. "Come on down here," Lettie told him. "You done found Maud Free."

Folks were there. Boxcars. Sliding doors rolled open. Folks, children, came forward. Women, smiling at him. Boys and girls, coming close.

"Well you come, Maud Free," they murmured.

"Where she be?" he asked softly. He knew how to speak above a whisper. Mary had showed him that. "Where, Mary?"

The children looked all around them expectantly. One woman who seemed to be in charge of him took him by the hand. "So happy you are here. Well you come!" she said.

"Thank-y," he answered, the way he knew how.

"You gone be busy!" she told him, smiling. "You and Maybrey here, you all can do everything. You all can learn together!"

They kept him so busy, learning and seeing. Children rushed around him, doing chores, sometimes playing. He learned some of their names. He ate so much food.

Maybrey took his arm. Maybrey found some of his own clothes for Luke. Brogans that fit him. All his worn and worn-out clothes were put in the washing, and later hung to dry. He and Maybrey tore the worn-out ones into rags after they dried.

Late in the day, he bathed in a tub of hot water and washed his hair. Maybrey was there to hand him soap and a towel. Hand him Maybrey's own clothes. The clothes weren't new, he could tell. But they were clean hand-me-downs. Maybrey was polite; careful not to look at him as he dressed.

After his bath, Luke worked some more. Not too hard, but work that would build him up, Rassela, Maybrey's mama, told him. "Fetch coal and wood from the coal and wood pile," Rassela told him. "For to heat the stoves in our houses."

"No houses!" he told Maybrey when they were at work by themselves. "They boxcars. How you folks get some boxcars?"

"Long time ago," Maybrey told. "Minister man

lived in the South come here. He bought some land. Then he went down south again, brought some-us up to here. He had some-us move into goods wagons, what they call 'em in Eng-land where he went to school. Goods wagons were great strong wagons for the railway and already here."

Luke wanted to talk some, but Maybrey never gave him the chance. Maybrey went on, working fast with his hands, tossing coal into wheelbarrows. Hands, black with coal dust. Luke did the same. Careful to keep their clothes clean.

"He made goods wagons into people houses," Maybrey explained. "Two houses to a wagon. He put a cookstove and a heat stove in each house."

"First to come here with him was his Tunny Maud," Maybrey told. "His property gave over from his papa. Say she was a real little person. Say she could sing and dance and swing from trees, like a monkey.

"She looked around, Tunny Maud did, eyed him, saying, 'No Tunny Maud, callen me. No more. This day, every one, callen me *Tunnee Free*, till I die.' Well, we guess they did call her that for a while. People couldn't say the name the way she could. So, see, they combined her name to this place. Calling it Maud Free. It was easier for folks, Maud Free was, more than Tunnee, or Tunny, or whatever she called herself. And Maud Free stuck to this place.

"And him, minister man, he let 'em all go. All his once-property. He brought 'em all north. All his men carrying guns. Sometimes, he drove his once-property down the middle of the streets through the South, getting here. His men had whips, like they was driving slaves to someplace else.

"But it was pretend time. They'd pretend to whip Tunnee Maud with a snapping whip. Then she would dance and walk on her hands. But she'd do that anyway. That's how they got his property out of dangerous white countryside. Pretend to whip slaves down the street, and townsfolks laughing and egging him and his men on. Sometimes they'd find a train ride, but they had to keep their guns in the open for show. People didn't like seeing the black folks ride the trains. But once passed Baltimore and into Cincinnati, they were almost home free.

"She gone now," Maybrey went on in his singsong voice. "African woman out of the Con-go! Say she stand a long time among trees and talk to the leaves. Paste the leaves all over her. Say she treat trees like people. She pat them and laugh."

Maybrey could talk forever. Young Luke didn't mind.

Two days passed. Luke slept in a room with boys in one boxcar. Funny to him, to sleep in a great big box. But he slept well, on a straw mattress. He was tired from days of walking and riding. And he was warm. Warm! He worked in Maud Free even when tired. And slowly he got stronger and less tired.

Maud Free was a good-sized town now. Hadn't been just a woman's name for a long time now. But a town full of people who looked like him and Maybrey. He found out their land was a hundred acres shared among them. They did most everything for themselves. Every boxcar had a cow and a horse or two. Had a fenced pasture. Had a gate. The land that was Maud Free had sheds and farmers and wrought-iron workers. Had huts made of straw and clay and such, round houses, like in Africa. Old practice taught by Tunnee Free, long ago. Kept hams and bacon, mutton, too, in the round houses. Round houses made of twigs and branches and stuff. They were good summer places, but not good enough for hard winters, Maybrey said.

Every boxcar had vegetables growing around it. Corn and pole beans and such. The fields were planted with corn for animals. Pumpkins for pies and to sell, barley, and soy. There were cow barns and pig sheds. They sold to villages around them. They had guns for hunting wild game. The men were careful to hunt only on their own land. They sold wild turkey in the markets. One or two of the men carried side arms, until told by the constable that they shouldn't.

"But Maud Free," they told him. They were men of few words.

"Just a year more, then you leave firearms at home," the constable said.

Still, they were ever watchful. Yet nobody bothered them. They were a lot of black folks, keeping to themselves.

They could buy stuffs from stores when they had to. They bought cotton ticking for mattress covers. But they made their own monk's cloth for curtains and bedcovers. They made candy, but they bought some, too. They bought some candles. They bought saws and hammers.

It was the middle of the second night when Luke sat straight up in bed and howled like an animal. Swiftly, Maybrey leaped to Luke and covered his mouth.

"Don't yell again," Maybrey whispered. "People tired. Don't be causing them worry over you."

When Maybrey thought Luke was ready to calm down, he carefully removed his hand from Luke's face. Again, Luke started a howl. Maybrey sat on his chest and knocked the wind out of him. He got up and kneeled by the bed, his hand at the ready.

Luke lay there with his mouth open. It was an awful, sickening feeling for him, not being able to breathe.

He held on to his stomach and swallowed. Sweat popped out on his forehead.

"No, you don't be sick! No, you don't!"

Maybrey warned him. "Don't worry, your breath's coming back. But there's nothing for it, don't you know? It took you long enough to notice. But she be gone, son. Your mama's gone."

Luke lay there, breathing as if the next breath might be his last. Shaking now, and afraid. How could he have not noticed? How could it have happened? She was his mother. She left him.

"'Cause of you!" Luke accused Maybrey. "You just wouldn't stop talking. Wouldn't leave me be. This place too big!"

"Don't blame nobody else," Maybrey said. Evenly, softly. "I din't do it, and you din't do it. Lotsa folks go when they has to, just like that old African. Had her own business to tend to in the worries outside. So she left one day. Say she wasn't even four feet tall. And went off on her own. Prolly all the way back to the Con-go! Hee, hee!"

"No," Luke whispered. "I hate Maud Free!"

"Old African woman make the mazes," Maybrey said.

"What mazes?" Luke asked.

"You don't even know," Maybrey told. "Your mama follow the African's maze to come by here. Old Tunnee Free left here many times, they say, to bring runaways out of the forest. Say bounty men hunted for her, but she could be invisible among the leaves, just so. But one last time, she went for good. Went way back to her forest across the water."

CHAPTER FIFTEEN

A Maze

"Ahhh!" Valena sighed. "Amazing!" she murmured. And sat up, in surprise. They were under the old maple.

She didn't remember dragging a chair out of the sun. Her mom must've moved them to the shade of the tree. She did remember moving, though, like in a dream. She had been so deep in the time of her Graw Luke.

She was all the way forward to now, though, in an instant. Feeling the heat of this time of day.

Three or four o'clock, she guessed. The clouds were gathering into high white thunderheads.

Her mom could tell about things, all right. Things full of pictures that Valena could see. What she couldn't quite see or understand, she could imagine, or question.

"But what was a maze?" she asked now.

"Some called the Underground Railroad a maze," her mom said. "Which wasn't a railroad either," her mom added. "You know that."

"It was places to hide and ways to go," Valena said. "Right? And anywhere they could go and be safe."

"*They*," her mom said, "were *our* folks, and other Occupants, running for their lives."

"But Mom, how did you know all that? You weren't there. Who told you?"

"Why, it came down, is all," Harriet said. "It's the family truth. Maybe we didn't hear all the words. See all the expressions and feel the cold and the hurt. But we know what it was like back then. We know, and we can tell it like it was. We find the words, and we write it down, too.

"It first came down from Graw Luke himself," she said. "First story I ever heard from my own dad. He told me that Graw Luke sat down his many children once a year. He told them of his early life. About running away and finding Maud Free."

"Yes," Valena said. And then she got it. "Your dad was Luke's son!"

Her mom nodded. "He was Worthy Harper, yes." She hurried on, as though once she began, she didn't want to stop.

"But remember, I told you things always change. And the settlement of Maud Free was bound to change, too. Folks left the boxcars, finally. They learned to build houses for themselves. Some even quit farming. Some of them moved away. The needs of people changed. They didn't have to live separate. Separate themselves from other people. And after his mother left him, Graw Luke stayed long enough to learn more than one trade. He could farm, black-smith, and bricklay. We don't know exactly how he felt. But probably he had hardened himself, quieted himself."

"And he left?" Valena asked. "That little boy left?"

"After he grew some," her mom explained. "At seventeen, he moved away to another town. He stayed by himself, working here and there. Years later, he met the woman he would marry. She was a farm woman named Maydell Worth. We talk mostly about Graw Luke because he's the one that told about his life. And he went out to work in the powder mill, and he got burned when the mill blew."

"Wow!" Valena said softly. "Goodness sakes."

Her mom didn't talk much more that day.

Over time, that summer, Valena learned most of what there was to know about all the times of her family.

She found out Maydell Worth had been a nice woman. She did her chores and cared for her babies. She grew crops. She was as strong as her husband — she enjoyed her life and her three children.

It was sad when Valena found out what happened to her mom's parents. They died too soon, in a car accident. It was something Valena's mom never talked about. And it was the reason neither Valena's father nor mother drove an automobile. Maybe, in one of Simony's notebooks, there was a Reckoning about it.

All summer, Valena felt full of times that were not her own — even as she was having her own times and memories. There was just so much, she thought. Some very good, some awfully bad. At times, she felt full to bursting.

Things stayed different.

It's the summer of Laddie and Luke, she told herself. *Now why do I put a dog and a man together? Because. I love them both.*

She felt the hurt in losing Laddie. And the pain of being born too late for Luke. *It's so sad I never knew Luke. Never carried wood with him, or ate with him.*

The boy, Luke, my Great-Graw Luke! Change times, and she imagined she and young Luke could've been friends. He wouldn't've been so alone.

Well, goodness! she thought. It always had been — the dog and the man. Right! Laddie and her own dad. So why not Laddie and Luke? One time and another. One kind of just terrible and another kind of awful.

Valena slept until two in the afternoon. The house was quiet. Nobody bothered her. She got up when her sunny room became too hot to take.

None of them were the same, though, in her

house. They all missed Laddie. She felt it as she roamed through the summertime. Seemed like it all got mixed up in the story of the boy Luke. The loss of so many. *Somehow*, she thought, *the boy, Luke, and I walk the same lonely line.* She couldn't quite see herself and Tunnee Maud. They weren't kin, though. Strange how Tunnee found her way into their past. By her name becoming Luke's own first home place. Tunnee Maud Free! *She's an example, though,* Valena thought. *A model for carrying on.*

In the now, even Adam was different without Laddie to pet or run with. Adam would start something. He hit Valena once in a while on her arm, to raise a goose bump, and it hurt. She told her mom.

Adam didn't actually stop it or say he was sorry. He left the house early and came back late. Mostly, Valena stayed out of his way. "Let him grow up," her mom told her.

When's that going to be? she wondered.

Her dad came down the road alone at evening. Quietly stepping in the yard and putting his arm around her to walk to the porch.

She was lonesome without Laddie in the yard waiting for the time for her dad to come home. Even Babysis seemed distant and different.

Valena couldn't understand how young Luke's mom could leave him like that. She sat on her bike under the maple all alone. But she didn't ride it until she thought to ride it around the yard. Around and around she went, as if making a circle could make Laddie come back. Or take her to Luke's time. When she thought that, she dropped the bike and retreated to the porch steps.

For she'd had a further thought — *bring my mom's mom and dad back.* But then that made her think of ghosts. She shivered and felt ashamed of herself.

Melinda came by. Came speeding into the yard and slid on the grass to a stop right in front of Valena. "Wanna go for a ride?" she asked.

"No, I don't," Valena said. She had her elbow propped up on her knee and her hand under her chin. She was looking over Melinda's head. But she was sure glad to see her.

"You're still mad at me for going to camp," Melinda said.

"You left me all alone," Valena told her. *Just like Luke's mom left him.*

"No I didn't," Melinda said. "I went to camp, was all."

"Well . . ." Valena was silent a good long while. Melinda sat on her bike, holding on to the handlebars the whole time.

"They say Bobby Tousons and his family are moving to Oklahoma."

"No! No!" Valena rose up.

"That's what I heard," Melinda said. "They lost their farm somehow. They didn't like it here much anyway. That's what people say. They have relatives out in Oklahoma or Nevada, someplace."

Valena sat down hard. *That's just awful*, she thought, and buried her face in her arms.

After a while, Melinda said gently, "We could ride out there and say good-bye."

Finally, Valena answered. "I never knew him very well. Anyway, I'm not riding my bike anymore."

"Oh, Valena, why?"

"Because I don't want to. I'm not riding to sixth grade at all. I'm walking!"

"Well, we can. It's not that far. I don't mind," Melinda said.

"We're getting too old for bikes," Valena said, looking up, then putting her head down on her arms again. She knew that wasn't true.

They stayed in their positions until quietly Melinda put her bike on the ground and climbed the steps to sit beside Valena. Melinda could hear

Valena sniffling. She sat there, holding her ankles and resting her back. Waiting.

It was a while before Valena stopped. She lifted her head and wiped her eyes.

"I don't even have a hankie," Melinda said. "You want me to go in and get you one?"

"No, that's okay," Valena answered. "Thanks, though."

"You wanna walk some?" her cousin asked.

Valena heaved a sigh. "Yes."

They got up and left the yard. They walked together up the street; they crossed the street and headed down the road toward Melinda's house.

They walked casually, learning the right pace in the heat. "It's nice to walk," Valena said. She could feel her arms in a different way. "Walking to sixth grade might be nice."

"Yeah," Melinda said. They walked with the same rhythm.

"We walk just alike," Valena said, surprised.

"We're cousins," Melinda said, matter-of-factly.

"You ever know about Graw Luke?" Valena asked — all of a sudden.

"Sure," Melinda said.

"My mom just told me," Valena said.

"Well. They tell you when you are way little; then they tell you again when you're older," Melinda told her.

"That's funny! Why is that?"

Melinda was grinning at her. "They want it to sink way in your head!"

They laughed. "Is it true? He ran away and found Maud Free?" Valena asked.

"Yeah," Melinda said. "And he ran away from Maud Free and found — himself!"

"Is that right?"

"Well, I think so," Melinda said. "He grew up and bought a farm and had a family."

"So I guess he did," Valena said, finally. *I guess he did just what he wanted. He found himself,* she thought.

They walked through the heat of the day.

Valena thought to say, "All kinds of sad things happen to people, you know? My mom lost her parents in a car accident."

"I know," Melinda said. And then, they fell silent.

I must've known about it, Valena thought. *They must've told me when I was too young to remember.* Valena found that, like her mom, she didn't much want to talk about it to anyone. Somehow it was too close, too near.

She and Melinda talked about the sound of insects, rising and falling in unison. "Wonder how do they know how to do that?" Melinda asked.

"Just born in them, I guess," Valena said.

They talked about all kinds of accidents. Laddie and even Tunnee Maud had been an accident in the life of the family. They walked to Melinda's house, under the big chinaberry trees and inside, to the dining room. The big oak table was there. Always had been. Valena sat down at one end of the table.

Melinda got them lemonade. They were each at an end of the table, with a glass. They drank and swallowed and sighed. And finally, they reached out across the table to each other.

"Oh my goodness!" Valena said.

"Oh, I don't believe it," Melinda said.

For the first time they could reach each other's hands across the table. They hadn't been able to before.

"Have we grown?"

"Let's see!"

In the kitchen, on the wall, were markings. Aunt Demmie came in from outside, saw what they were doing. She found a pencil. And measured each of their heads on the wall. "Well, I'll be," she said.

"We've grown!" Valena said.

"I grew the most," Melinda said.

"Well, I don't mind." Valena found she really didn't mind. "Things always change, so we have to, too."

They left the house. "I'll walk you back," Melinda said.

"Then who'll walk *you* back? You'll stay for supper," Valena decided.

"We'll sleep out tonight!" Melinda said.

"Right! We'll call your mom."

They walked back, complaining of the heat.

"Will sixth grade be hard, you think?" Valena asked.

"Probably," Melinda said, like it was nothing.

"I'll probably get some bad grades, too," Valena said.

"No, you won't. You're a Harper."

Valena stopped and stared at her cousin. "I never thought of that!" she said. "I mean, but I'm a McGill *and* a Harper! I'm a Harper like Graw Luke. Like his children and my mom! I'm a Harper all the time!

"Let's run!" Valena yelled. And they did.

"You always beat me, running," Melinda called from somewhere behind her.

"I know it," Valena said, breathing easily. She ran in long strides. And stopped suddenly, when she remembered Melinda's birthday was coming. "August nineteenth." She bowed in front of her cousin, who came up breathing hard. She pretended she was Tunnee Maud. She danced and sang; managed a crooked handstand for a few seconds.

"Happy Birthday — soon — to YOU-UUUU!" Valena sang, falling over backwards.

"Yeah!" Melinda caught her before she hit the blacktop.

And that was that.

The End

A NOTE ABOUT
THIS BOOK

Time Pieces: The Book of Times began as a collection of loosely connected scenes and stories, many of which occurred at various times in Virginia Hamilton's life. Others were drawn from stories Ms. Hamilton had been told by her family about her grandfather's escape from slavery in Virginia to freedom in Ohio. When he was a child, Ms. Hamilton's grandfather, Levi Perry, was led by his mother, Mary Cloud, along the Underground Railroad to Ohio.

In "The Greatest," Ms. Hamilton presents

both fiction and autobiography. Gargantua the Great toured with Ringling Bros. and Barnum & Bailey in 1938 until the animal died in 1949. Ms. Hamilton's dad took her to see Gargantua when the circus came to Dayton, Ohio, in 1947 or 1948—some thirty years before the character of Valena McGill enters the picture!

Ms. Hamilton did some time-skating here because she felt the story was such a good one. The fiction brings Gargantua and Valena together in the same time frame by placing a fictional character, Valena, who was not part of the event, next to a famous being, who was. Thus, we have Valena McGill seeing the great ape Gargantua.

Ms. Hamilton stated that she remembered everything about seeing the magnificent animal. And she wanted her readers to experience the extraordinary fictional and true story through Valena's eyes.

The final draft of *Time Pieces: The Book of*

Times was completed the week before Thanksgiving 2001. The manuscript had been significantly revised by Ms. Hamilton during the previous eight months and had been expanded by nearly twenty-five percent. In a note accompanying the revised manuscript, Ms. Hamilton wrote to her editor, Bonnie Verburg, "Good day, Bonfire! Hope you'll enjoy. I certainly had a ball writing it. Have a fine Thanksgiving. We go to my niece's. I make the turkey and stuffing. Yummy."

Virginia Hamilton died of breast cancer less than three months later, on February 19, 2002.

PARTIAL HARPER/MCGILL
FAMILY TREE

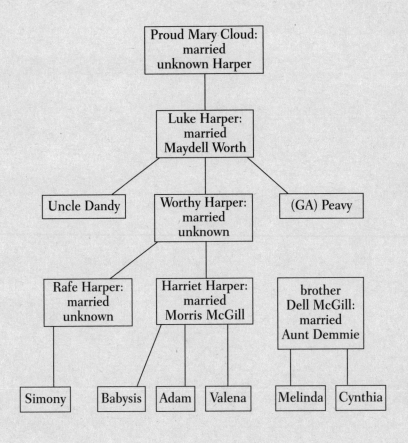

ALSO BY
VIRGINIA HAMILTON

Zeely
(New York: Macmillan, 1969)

The House of Dies Drear
(New York: Macmillan, 1969)

The Time-Ago Tales of Jahdu
(New York: Macmillan, 1969)

The Planet of Junior Brown
(New York: Macmillan, 1971)

W. E. B. Du Bois: A Biography
(New York: Crowell, 1972)

Time-Ago Lost: More Tales of Jahdu
(New York: Macmillan, 1973)

M. C. Higgins, the Great
(New York: Macmillan, 1974)

Paul Robeson:
The Life and Times of a Black Man
(New York: Harper & Row, 1974)

The Writings of W. E. B. Du Bois
edited by Hamilton (New York: Crowell, 1975)

Arilla Sun Down
(New York: Greenwillow, 1976)

Illusion and Reality
(Washington, D. C.: Library of Congress, 1976)

Justice and Her Brothers
(New York: Greenwillow, 1978)

Dustland
(New York: Greenwillow, 1980)

Jahdu
(New York: Greenwillow, 1980)

The Gathering
(New York: Greenwillow, 1981)

Sweet Whispers, Brother Rush
(New York: Philomel, 1982)

The Magical Adventures of Pretty Pearl
(New York: Harper & Row, 1983)

Willie Bea and the Time the Martians Landed
(New York: Greenwillow, 1983)

A Little Love
(New York: Philomel, 1984)

Junius Over Far
(New York: Harper & Row, 1985)

The People Could Fly:
American Black Folktales
(New York: Knopf, 1985)

The Mystery of Drear House:
The Conclusion of the Dies Drear Chronicle
(New York: Greenwillow, 1987)

A White Romance
(New York: Philomel, 1987)

Anthony Burns:
The Defeat and Triumph of a Fugitive Slave
(New York: Knopf, 1988)

In the Beginning:
Creation Stories from Around the World
(San Diego: Harcourt Brace Jovanovich, 1988)

The Bells of Christmas
(San Diego: Harcourt Brace Jovanovich, 1989)

The Dark Way: Stories from the Spirit World
(San Diego: Harcourt Brace Jovanovich, 1990)

Cousins
(New York: Philomel, 1991)

The All Jahdu Storybook
(San Diego: Harcourt Brace Jovanovich, 1991)

Drylongso
(San Diego: Harcourt Brace Jovanovich, 1992)

Many Thousand Gone:
African Americans from Slavery to Freedom
(New York: Knopf, 1993)

Plain City
(New York: The Blue Sky Press/Scholastic, 1993)

Her Stories: African American Folktales,
Fairy Tales, and True Tales
(New York: The Blue Sky Press/Scholastic, 1995)

Jaguarundi
(New York: The Blue Sky Press/Scholastic, 1995)

When Birds Could Talk & Bats Could Sing:
The Adventures of Bruh Sparrow,
Sis Wren, and Their Friends
(New York: The Blue Sky Press/Scholastic, 1996)

A Ring of Tricksters:
Animal Tales from America,
the West Indies, and Africa
(New York: The Blue Sky Press/Scholastic, 1997)

Second Cousins
(New York: The Blue Sky Press/Scholastic, 1998)

Bluish
(New York: The Blue Sky Press/Scholastic, 1999)

The Girl Who Spun Gold
(New York: The Blue Sky Press/Scholastic, 2000)

For more about Virginia Hamilton,
please visit her Web site at www.virginiahamilton.com.

Newbery Medalist

VIRGINIA HAMILTON

(1936–2002)

was one of the most distinguished writers of our time, and this final draft of *Time Pieces,* a semi-autobiographical novel, was finished shortly before her death. Like Valena, Ms. Hamilton grew up in farm country surrounded by an extended family and generations of storytellers. Her grandfather, Levi Perry, was brought by his mother, Mary Cloud, from Virginia slavery to Ohio via the Underground Railroad.

Ms. Hamilton received nearly every award in the field of children's literature, including the international Hans Christian Andersen Medal, the John Newbery Medal, the Laura Ingalls Wilder Medal, the Coretta Scott King Award, the *Boston Globe–Horn Book* Award, the Edgar Allan Poe Award, the Regina Medal, and the Ohioana Award. Three of her books were Newbery Honor Books, and she was the first writer of children's books to receive a MacArthur Fellowship. *Time Pieces* was her twenty-first novel.

Praise for
VIRGINIA HAMILTON'S
Time Pieces

"Drawing in part from her own memories, the late, much-honored author takes a child through a summer of high times and low, of anxious moments and long, lazy days, of loss, love, laughter, and strengthening ties to the past. . . . Written in Hamilton's usual distinctive, creamy idiom, these episodes move back and forth in time, capturing a child finding her place amid those of generations past and present. . . . The first (one hopes not the last) of Hamilton's works to appear posthumously, this makes a loving, thoughtful addition to her unique literary legacy."

— *Kirkus Reviews*

"Using her fine gift of storytelling, Hamilton creates intriguing characters and a unique tale that floats on the edges of reality. . . . This book will be best enjoyed by careful, thoughtful readers."

— *Voice of Youth Advocates*

"A number of interconnected 'reckons,' . . . stories told of past times . . . are polished like prized gems that are passed down from one generation to the next."

— *Publishers Weekly*

"As always with Hamilton, the telling is the story. Her fans will also be fascinated to see the seeds of so many of her books here, from *The People Could Fly* (1985) to *Cousins* (1990)."

— *Booklist*

"Hamilton knows how mysterious the unknown can be to children, and has a superb ear for dialogue. . . . The simplicity and directness of the language serve the subject matter beautifully."

— *School Library Journal*

Other books by
VIRGINIA HAMILTON

Arilla Sun Down

Bluish

Cousins

Second Cousins

The Mystery of Drear House

Plain City

A White Romance

The Justice Cycle:
Justice and Her Brothers (Book One)
Dustland (Book Two)
The Gathering (Book Three)